I0588957

Down River

Doug Fletcher book 7

Dean L. Hovey

Print ISBNs
BWL Print 9780228615606
Amazon Print 9780228615613
B&N Print 9780228615620
LSI Print 9780228616726

BWL Publishing Inc.

Books we love to write ...
Authors around the world.
http://bwlpublishing.ca

Dedication

To Mike and Maria Westfall

I must thank many people for their assistance. Julie, my wife, offered opinions and critiques of the medical terminology. Fran Brozo, Dan Fouts, and Mike Westfall offered ideas, critiques, and constructive suggestions to improve the story and details. Anne Flagge and Natalie Lund proofread and corrected typos, grammar, and punctuation. Thanks to Deanna Wilson, who stepped into the law enforcement consultant's role, offering corrections and suggestions about police procedures and the plot. Many thanks to Susan Davis and Jude Pittman of BWL for your editing, assistance, and support.

"I've dipped a canoe paddle into crystal clear waters as the sun rose, hearing only the call of loons and splash of jumping fish. At that moment, I realized I was in God's greatest cathedral."

D. L. Hovey

Chapter One

Friday

Janet Eastman sat in the front seat of the canoe, and her new husband, Dave, took the back as they glided down the St. Croix River. They let the moderate current carry them slowly, with Dave taking an occasional paddle stroke to keep them away from deadfalls and rocks, and out of the center of the waterway. They skirted small islands, scaring up ducks, and disturbing two great blue herons, wading the shallow water searching for fish.

Janet reached behind her seat and took a bottle of sunscreen out of the bag. She slathered cream on her arms, torso, and legs, then tossed the bottle to Dave.

"You'd better refresh your sunscreen, dear, or you'll look like a boiled lobster by the time we get to the outfitter's pickup point."

Unlike Janet, whose mother was Vietnamese, Dave was Scandinavian/Irish, redheaded, and blue-eyed. Without copious layers of sunscreen, he would, indeed, look like a lobster by the end of the day. He slipped off his life jacket, took the bottle, squeezed out a blob of cream, and rubbed it on his freckled face and arms. Between the sunscreen application and watching Janet take off her life jacket and adjust her bikini bra to get sunscreen on every potentially exposed skin area, he was distracted.

He set his paddle inside the canoe and knelt forward. "You missed your back," he said playfully. Reaching out with his right hand full of cream, he leaned on the left gunwale. The canoe rocked, and Janet jumped with surprise as the cool sunscreen unexpectedly hit her back.

The canoe scraped over a submerged rock, and the combination of the rock, Janet's quick move, and Dave shifting the center of gravity, caused the canoe to tip left. Janet and Dave both leaned right to counteract the motion, causing the canoe to flip over after it passed the rock. They were thrown into the water, losing their paddles and life jackets.

Dave came up sputtering and quickly reached for the canoe. Janet, farther away, had no problem swimming a few strokes to the canoe. She grabbed the bag with their water and lunch, prioritizing it over the nearby life jacket and paddle that drifted away in the current. They tried to get back into the canoe but only filled it with water.

They kicked, pushing the canoe toward shore, then found footing in the soft river silt. Getting themselves and the canoe near shore, they took stock of their situation. Dave's paddle still lay inside the canoe, but Janet's paddle and their life jackets had drifted downstream. The island was tiny and overgrown, unlike many of the other islands that had small sandy beaches and appeared more park-like due to the canoeists who stopped to picnic and camp.

Janet caught her breath after they pulled the canoe into reeds. "What now?"

"Let's tip the canoe and dump the water. I can keep us in the current with one paddle. It'll take a while to get to our pickup spot, but I doubt the outfitter will leave without us."

A small fishing boat putted upstream toward them. The two fishermen had their poles out and were trolling.

Janet waved her arms. "Let's see if they'll take us down to the pickup spot."

"I think we can make it ourselves."

Janet continued to wave. "Maybe they'll at least get the other paddle and our life jackets."

The fishermen saw her waving and reeled in their lures before turning the boat to cross the open channel toward them.

"You two need a hand?"

"Yes," Janet gasped. "Can you help us get to our pickup spot? We capsized and lost one of our paddles and life jackets."

The fisherman in the back of the boat eyed Janet's skimpy bikini, then looked at Dave. Both were scraped and muddy. "Yeah. Push that canoe farther on shore, and we'll help you tie it up. Then we'll see if we can find your other paddle."

Dave looked at the men and felt uneasy. "Why don't you two keep fishing. We've got this."

The man in the back smiled. "No. It's the law of the seas. Boaters have to help each other." Although still early morning, the man in the back lifted a beer can to his lips and finished off the can. Then he threw it into the water.

Janet frowned. "That's not allowed here. The outfitter told us to pack out our trash."

The man pulled another beer from the cooler, and their boat bumped into the canoe. He popped the tab and took another drink. "Someone'll take care of it. There's lots of 'do-gooders' out here."

Janet looked at Dave and saw his apprehension. "Yeah, my husband's right. We don't need your help. Thanks anyway."

The man in the front was younger and agile. He stepped from the boat to the canoe, then onto the shore. He put out his hand to Janet, who was standing in knee-deep water. "Here, let me help you ashore."

Janet shook her head. "No, I think we've got this under control."

While Janet focused on the younger man, she'd turned away from Dave until she heard a dull thud and a splash. She looked back. Dave floated facedown in the water. The older man stood in the boat, holding an oar like a baseball bat.

Chapter Two

Monday

Jill and I were barely out of her air-conditioned pickup and into the muggy Texas heat when my boss, Matt Mattson, the superintendent of Padre Island National Seashore, waved to us from the park headquarters building.

Jill smiled at me. "What have you done this time?"

"Why is it *me* who's done something? I'm not always in trouble."

"You're in trouble more often than I am."

I was sweaty from the walk across the parking lot. I rode my fat tire bike alongside Jill on her daily beach runs, but she also worked out three times a week in the health club. Her workout regimen and trim figure apparently left her unfazed by the heat, while mild exertion left me dripping with sweat. We found Matt in his office. Jill stood in his doorway, and I sat in one of his guest chairs. I acted innocent of whatever infraction I'd committed, but Jill's question had my mind searching for something I'd done to earn chastisement by the boss. "What's up?"

Matt gestured for Jill to sit, and he closed his office door. I grinned at Jill. "It's not me this time."

"What's not you?" Matt asked as he sat.

"Jill suggested I was in trouble over something I'd done."

Matt reached for his printer and handed me a sheet of paper. "Have either of you ever been on a canoe trip?"

Jill leaned against my shoulder so she could read the email Matt had given me.

"I went on a Minnesota Boundary Waters camping trip and I canoed the Namekagon River as a scout. But that was thirty years ago." The email was a broadcast to all park superintendents asking them to identify law enforcement rangers who had experience canoeing. I handed the email to Jill, who scanned it and gave it back to me.

"I've canoed lakes a few times and taken a white-water rafting tour, but I've never been in a canoe on a river."

I handed the email back to Matt. "We're a little long in the tooth for a canoe adventure. I'm sure there are young rangers with more experience in canoes than Jill and me."

Matt set the email back on his printer. His sly smile made me uneasy. "I called the superintendent of the St. Croix National Scenic Riverway to see what she was looking for. She'd been contacted by the Secret Service and asked to provide rangers to help with security while the President's son is on a canoe trip with his school."

I tried to envision pictures of the President and his family. I'd seen them hustling across the White House lawn toward the Marine helicopter and had the impression the son was a young teenager.

Jill answered my unasked question. "I read that he's just celebrated his thirteenth birthday."

"That sounds about right," Matt said.

I started to get up, thinking we'd successfully evaded the assignment, but Matt motioned for me to sit. "Cheryl Britton is the superintendent of the St. Croix National Scenic Riverway. She's got lots of rangers who canoe. But she doesn't have any seasoned law enforcement rangers nor anyone with investigative experience."

I glanced at Jill, who seemed as lost as I was. "Okay. What's a lack of investigators got to do with protecting the President's kid?"

"A newlywed couple went canoeing on the St. Croix River and didn't return. Their canoe was recovered in Stillwater, about twenty miles south from where the outfitter dropped them. The National Park Service wants to know what happened to them before the Secret Service shows up." Matt looked at me. "You grew up in Minnesota, and you were a St. Paul cop. Isn't that close to Stillwater?"

"I've been to Stillwater but not for the canoeing. I remember it as a busy tourist town where cars got backed up every weekend with people driving back and forth over a two-lane bridge to their Wisconsin cabins. It's been decades since I've been there."

"You used to work with Mark Guertin, right?"

I had to dig deep in my memory. "Yeah, Mark and I worked out of the same St. Paul substation when we were rookie cops. Why do you ask?"

"He's the Stillwater Police chief and he's got a detective assigned to this investigation. He'd like you to call."

Jill and I made an offer on a Port Aransas house and were awaiting the seller's response to our offer. We were putting down roots, and I'd been warned by other rangers that buying a home was a dangerous financial proposition when you worked for the National Park Service. I had a bad feeling about where this was going.

"I'm not moving back to Minnesota."

Matt smiled. "Cheryl only wants you long enough to complete the investigation. Your home park will remain here."

"You make it sound like this is a done deal."

"You can say no but having stepped in a canoe and your investigative credentials put you at the top of the list for this."

Jill put her hand on my arm. "It's okay. I'll be fine here."

I looked at Jill. "Are you okay dealing with the realtor on your own?"

Matt interrupted. "Cheryl would like both of you."

Jill frowned. "Why?"

"She was vague about that, but she said she'd prefer a female investigator or a male/female team."

Jill looked at the door to make sure it was closed and leaned forward, speaking softly. "I've been around long enough to know that means she's got a problem with her staff. It's hard enough to focus on investigating anything without dealing with whatever is going on among your rangers."

Matt picked up a pen and rolled it between his fingers. "Understanding that is why you're the perfect person to accompany Doug on this trip."

Jill leaned back. "I was looking forward to ending my career here, quietly letting you deal with any of the personnel issues. I'm really not interested in getting embroiled in whatever's going on there."

"Jill, you may be the best person in the National Park Service to deal with this dual role. You're savvy, cool-headed, and experienced with personnel issues."

I smiled. "Sounds like you want Jill, and I can stay here to deal with the realtor."

Matt looked between us. "You're a team, and you've proven the value of you being together on an investigation."

Jill looked like she'd just sucked a lemon. She shook her head. "I vote no."

Matt pulled open his desk drawer and reached inside. He pushed a small black box across the desktop to Jill. She reluctantly lifted the lid, then set it back down, pushing the box back to Matt.

"Uh, uh. I'm just adjusting to my law enforcement role. You can't entice me with the 'investigator' title."

"The regional superintendent suggested that transition. He also suggested that you be sent to Glynco, Georgia, to the Federal Law Enforcement Training Class at the end of the assignment."

"Matt, I'm fifty-one years old. I have no interest in being put through school with a bunch of twenty-something kids who'll run my legs off and make me look like an old fool. Besides, by the time I'd get through the school, I'd be only five years away from mandatory retirement."

"Five years of service, from someone as seasoned as you, are worth twenty of some inexperienced kid. Besides, the National Park Service likes to team up the two of you."

Jill turned away and looked at the wall. "I don't think that's where I want to go at this point in my life."

Matt pushed the box back toward Jill. "I've been authorized to offer a carrot. If you accept an investigator's title and the two of you take this assignment, I can guarantee you won't be reassigned separately. You can finish your careers in Texas if that's what you want."

I put my hand on top of the box with the badge. "I've got news for you, Matt. We won't be reassigned to separate parks no matter what happens. Either or both of us can retire tomorrow, and I'd be happy to do that rather than splitting our assignments."

Jill looked at me. We'd always known that the specter of a National Park Service reassignment was out there, but we'd chosen to ignore it. The discussion had never made it to the table. In retrospect, that seemed naïve considering we'd made an offer on a house.

Jill lifted my hand off the box and picked it up, tapping it on Matt's desk. "Can we do this without me going to Glynco?"

Matt drew a deep breath. "I think it was meant to be more of a carrot than a stick. I can ask the question."

Jill pushed the box back to Matt. "Make the call. We'll get a cup of coffee."

I closed Matt's door as we left. "Are you sure you want to do this?"

Jill led me to the coffee pot, threw a quarter into the can, and poured us two cups. "I think the personnel issue in that park sounds fishy, and I'm not excited about stepping into someone else's mess. On the other hand, working investigations together for the next few years sounds intriguing."

"It's not glamorous, as you already know."

Jill sipped her coffee and thought. "Yes, but it beats spending the rest of my National Park Service career walking through the campground, chastising litterers, and driving the beach taking coins away from treasure hunters."

"I haven't been in a canoe in a long time, and it wasn't easy when I was sixteen."

"My only canoe experiences were on lakes in the Ozarks. I've never been on a river or seen rapids inside a canoe."

"As I recall, the St. Croix River is pretty placid most of its length."

Matt walked into the break area, smiling. "Book your flights." He handed Jill the investigator's badge and walked away.

I went to my office and looked up the phone number to call the Stillwater Police. Getting the front desk, I identified myself and asked for Chief Guertin as Jill brought two cups of fresh coffee into my office and closed the door.

"The chief is busy right now. Can I take a message?"

"Please ask him to call me at his earliest convenience." I gave the officer my name, title, office, and cellphone number.

Jill was doing something on her phone while I was talking. When I hung up, she handed me her phone. "Here's the phone number for the St. Croix National Scenic Waterway headquarters. Call the superintendent and let her know we're coming."

I pushed the phone across the desk. "She wanted a female investigator. She's probably more interested in talking to you than to me."

Jill didn't look happy, but she dialed the phone. She spoke with a ranger, then was put on hold. "She's away from her desk, and they're looking for her."

Jill switched the phone to speaker, and we listened to an instrumental Frank Sinatra song.

"This is Cheryl. How can I help you?"

"I'm Jill Fletcher at Padre Island National Seashore. I believe Matt Mattson spoke with you about an investigation."

"Hang on while I close the door." Cheryl was back in a few seconds. "Sorry about that, but there are a lot of people here this time of year. Yes, I spoke with Matt earlier this morning, and he said you and another investigator might be available for a temporary assignment."

"The other investigator is my husband, Doug, who's on speakerphone with me."

"Hi, Cheryl," I said. "What's going on up there?"

"I've got a hornet's nest. Between the Coast Guard, the Secret Service, two sheriffs' departments, the Stillwater Police, and National Park Service Human Resources, I'm drowning. Matt suggested I search for your names on the internet to get some background on your qualifications. I've got to say, Doug's been in the spotlight a couple times, and your combined investigative resumes are impressive. Matt said he was going to speak with you about my...situation. Are you guys available and interested in a short-term assignment?"

Jill leaned close to the phone. "We've been made available, but I've got to be honest, our canoeing experience is limited and dated. We can help with the investigative part of your problem, but please don't expect us to demonstrate any expertise on the water."

"Listen, Jill, the canoeing part of this is the least of my worries. I've got a bunch of seasonal rangers who are skilled canoeists, but I've got no one who's capable of investigating the disappearance of the missing couple. If you can strap on a life vest, I can put you in the front of a canoe with someone who'll skillfully get you anywhere on the river."

"Matt said you wanted a female investigator. Why?"

Cheryl paused so long I thought we'd lost the connection. "I've got a personnel problem among some of my rangers. I'd rather not get into it over the phone."

"You said something about National Park Service Human Resources being an issue. Are they involved?"

"Jill, you're from South Dakota, right? You've probably heard the phrase, 'having a burr under your blanket.'"

Jill looked at me with concern. "Yes, that's part of my ranch girl heritage."

"Well, that's where I'm at with Human Resources. A couple complaints have been lodged, and they're leaning on me to…resolve the problem without anyone involving the local police or filing a lawsuit."

I closed my eyes. "I assume there's an allegation of sexual impropriety."

"Doug, like I said, I'm not going into the details on the phone, but you're sniffing the right trail."

"I'll check flight options. We might be able to get there tomorrow night."

Jill put up her finger. "Cheryl, before we hang up, when did your canoeists disappear?"

"Their canoe was recovered in Stillwater yesterday, but they've been missing since Friday."

"Would it take two days for a canoe to drift to Stillwater?" I asked.

"Not if it was in the channel. We're assuming it was caught in some snags along the way." Cheryl paused. "The missing couple were on their honeymoon. Their wedding was just last Thursday."

"Is there some reason the local law enforcement people aren't jumping on this, and you feel you need more help?"

"The woman is my niece. My brother is crawling down my throat over this because I suggested the canoe trip and arranged for the outfitter. He's calling twice a day, and every evening he asks for updates. I've run out of excuses and...well, I need to do more than I'm getting out of the local folks."

I leaned close to the phone. "Are they classifying it as an accident or a missing persons case?"

"It's a presumptive drowning. I think they're waiting for the bodies to float down the river."

I hit the mute button. "It takes at least three days for a body to bloat and rise to the surface this time of year. This is about as early as I'd expect the authorities to recover a drowning victim."

"Are you still there?" Cheryl asked.

"Sorry, we were just discussing how to hand off our responsibilities here in Texas. I'll call the federal travel office and make reservations. One of us will get back to you as soon as we've nailed down our plans."

Cheryl's voice changed from sharply professional to troubled aunt. "Thank you. I…we need to get a handle on this."

I punched the button to end the call and looked at Jill. "This is going to be a hornet's nest of overlapping jurisdictions, personal and professional priorities, never minding whatever issue Cheryl's got with her rangers."

Jill searched my eyes. "You want to say no."

"Not really, but we need to be prepared to step lightly rather than barreling in like we're taking over."

"Your style isn't taking over. You've always worked closely with the local law enforcement people and shared the credit."

I leaned back. "This is different. The only person who wants us is Cheryl. I've got to assume all the other agencies think they've got this under control and that our presence will be an intrusion."

On cue, my desk phone rang. "This is Fletcher."

"Doug Fletcher, the former St. Paul cop?"

"Mark Guertin, how are you?"

Jill got up, but I waved her back into the chair.

"The dogs are nipping at my heels and I'm wearing Milk-Bone pants. How about you?"

"I'm a newlywed and working for the U.S. National Park Service, based in Texas."

"You're a Texan now? Man, that's a long way from Minnesota."

"It is, but I'm flying back. As a matter of fact, I've been asked to look into a National Park Service case that's going to overlap with you."

The lightness left Guertin's voice. "The drowning."

"Apparently, there are some people in the National Park Service who want us involved in the case. I'll be flying back this week with my partner. I'd like to talk to whoever you've assigned to the case to collect some background."

"It's not much of a case at this point. We found a canoe, and the people who rented it are missing. Sandy Prudhomme is the detective I've assigned to it, but it's just sitting on her desk until the bodies float up."

"You're treating it as a drowning?"

"I've got no reason to look at it any other way." Guertin paused then said, "You lived here, Doug. There are dozens of people who fall out of boats and canoes a year. Most are wearing life jackets and are rescued by other boaters, or they swim to shore. A percentage of the others drown."

"These two weren't wearing life jackets?"

"The Coast Guard Reserve found a life jacket with the outfitter's logo. It was hung up in tree branches along the river. The outfitter says the couple left with life jackets on but at least one of them took the life jacket off. You know how it goes; it was a hot July day, the river appears placid, you slip off your life jacket to work on your tan, and then something unexpected happens."

Jill raised her eyebrows, and I nodded my agreement with Mark's comments. "Hi, Chief Guertin. I'm Jill, Doug's partner. Do you have any reason to believe there was foul play?"

"I suggest you talk to Sandy. My knowledge of the case is limited. She can answer your questions." Guertin gave us Sandy Prudhomme's direct number.

"Mark, I don't want to step on your toes. We've been directed to get involved, but it's your case, and we're only there to support whatever your people are doing."

Guertin laughed. "That's what I hear from all the feds before they step all over my cases."

"Mark, we go back a long way. I promise that we'll be discreet and only aid whatever you're doing."

"I guess I'll have to believe you." Guertin's voice dropped the professional edge. "What have you been up to the last twenty years, Doug? I lost track of you."

"I was a detective and got injured during a foot chase. The department wanted to shove me in a corner with a computer, and I took a medical pension. I got divorced, crawled into a bottle for a while, then pulled up stakes and moved to Arizona. The National Park Service hired me as an investigator, and I've mostly been investigating deaths in national parks and monuments. I got transferred to Texas, got remarried, and I've been putting down roots near Corpus Christi."

Guertin laughed. "What fool did you find who'd marry a cynical, old, ex-alcoholic, divorced cop?"

Jill smiled and pulled the phone over. "Chief, this is Jill. I'm Doug's work and domestic partner."

"Oh, geez. I'm sorry if…"

"You don't need to apologize. I know about most of Doug's baggage, and it matches up well with the skeletons in my own closet. Can we buy you supper while we're up there? I'd like to hear some of the dirt Doug hasn't shared."

Guertin gave Jill his cellphone number. "Call me when you get settled here. I'd love to have supper with you. If I bring my wife, I'll share some of the sanitized versions of Doug's escapades."

"Sounds great, Chief!"

"I don't know what accommodations the National Park Service will cover, but there's a great little inn a block off Main Street that's cozy and has great meals. It's one of my wife's favorite spots for special dinners."

Jill added the name of the inn to the slip of paper with Mark's phone number. "Sounds great. We get per diem, and with our combined daily stipend, I'd think we should be able to afford more than a room at a national chain."

I disconnected the call and looked at Jill's note. "I'm fairly sure even our combined per diem won't cover an inn in downtown Stillwater. It's a trendy tourist area, and it's high season."

Jill folded the note. "This isn't up for discussion."

"But..."

"Do you remember our honeymoon?"

I thought back to the hubbub of visiting parents, the wrap up of a shooting investigation, delivering my mother to the airport the day after the wedding, and falling exhausted into our beds at the rental townhouse. There was no honeymoon, per se. "We spent a week in San Antonio when we first got to Texas."

"Get real, Fletcher," Jill said as she stood. "That was a stressful few days to find out if we could stand to be together. It was *not* a honeymoon. Book a room at the inn, and I really don't care if it costs more than our per diem."

"We have to call my mother."

Jill sat on my desk and looked at me earnestly. "I love Ronnie, but we aren't staying with her."

"I didn't say…"

Jill put up one finger. "How far is this inn from your mother's house?"

"Twenty miles or so."

Jill got up. "Perfect! Close enough so we can visit her, but not close enough so she'll just drop in unexpectedly."

"We stayed with your parents…"

"And you remember how that went. Did either of us get one good night's rest?"

I threw up my hands. I almost replied, yes dear, then remembered Jill's physical response to that phrase involving an elbow jabbed into my ribs. "I'll see what's possible."

Chapter Three

I called the National Park Service's travel bureau and was chastised for not making my travel plans two weeks in advance. "Your superintendent will get a notification of exception, and he or she will have to approve the extra expense."

"Here's his phone number. His name is Matt Mattson, and we've been dispatched to investigate a missing person."

"Sir, there's no need to be snarky. I'm just explaining the guidelines."

"I'm sorry to dump on you. I was told to get to Minneapolis as soon as possible. How do we make that happen?"

I heard keys clicking. "What's your departure airport?"

"Corpus Christi, Texas. Our destination is Minneapolis. I'll need a rental car and room reservations." I gave her the name of the inn suggested by Mark Guertin.

After a half-hour discussion about the cost and limited air service out of Corpus Christi, the cost advantages of using Wednesday departures, the high cost of rooms at the Stillwater Inn, and notification of the policy against male and female rangers sharing a hotel room, we were booked. I went in search of Jill to tell her we were on a 5 a.m. flight.

I found her on the steps outside the building using her cellphone. I was surprised that she'd already pinned the investigator badge to her shirt. She was smiling, and I heard her say, "Bye, Mom."

I held open the door and nodded inside the air-conditioned building. "Which Mom were you talking with?"

"Ronnie is excited that we're coming to Minnesota."

I closed my eyes. "I don't know how much time we'll have to spend with her. We're working on an investigation."

Jill smiled. "I'm sure we'll carve out some time. She said our timing was perfect. There's a Fletcher family reunion next weekend."

I groaned. "No way. I'm busy that day."

"I want to meet your relatives, and your mother is excited. I guess you haven't been to one of the annual reunions for years."

"There's a reason. Most of my relatives are people I'd prefer *not* to socialize with."

Jill hooked my elbow and steered me toward Matt's office. "You were on the phone for a long time. Did you make reservations?"

"We're booked on a 5 a.m. flight with connections through Dallas. We'll be in Minneapolis before 10 a.m."

Jill stopped. "We'll have to be at the airport at three o'clock."

I kept walking. "Yes. I hope Matt will drive or is willing to pay for an Uber."

Matt was on the phone but waved us in and pointed to his guest chairs. When the call ended, he closed the door. "Well, you've been busy, Doug. You pissed-off the travel office and asked for exceptions to at least three travel guidelines."

Jill's eyes went wide. "What did you do?"

Matt waved off her concern. "I approved your plane reservations and explained that you were married, which satisfied their concern about male and female rangers sharing a room. They're not happy that you've chosen the expensive Stillwater Inn but were reluctantly willing to accept that it was closer to your assignment and would save travel time. I have the opinion that saving your travel time was not a consideration over saving eighty dollars a night, but they let me approve it. I'm sure someone farther up the food chain is going to call and question my authorization, but that's okay."

"We're booked on a 5 a.m. departure flight. Can you drive us to the airport?"

Matt waited for me to say I was kidding. "You're serious?"

"Yes. We can drive ourselves, but the parking will cost almost as much as our hotel, and we'll have to leave the National Park Service pickup in the lot for a week."

Matt nodded. "We'll work something out."

* * *

Matt's car was idling at the curb at 2:30 a.m. when I opened the townhouse door. Matt's wife, Mandy, was driving and looked as much the southern belle as she did at cocktail hour. I slept at the gate, on the plane to Dallas, and in the terminal awaiting our Minneapolis flight.

Jill shook me and handed me a coffee. "Wake up and keep me company."

I stretched. "How long until our flight?"

"They said they'd start boarding in twenty minutes."

"What have you been doing while I slept?"

"I called the park and spoke with Cheryl Britton."

"She was there at…" I looked for a clock.

"I think she's there 24/7. She's a basket case. Between this being her park's busiest time of the year, the missing honeymoon couple, the undefined personnel issue, and the impending Secret Service visit, she's not getting any sleep. She's pleased that we're on our way, and she suggested that we give her a call once we're checked into our hotel."

"Did you tell her we're staying in Stillwater?"

"She was disappointed we wouldn't be closer to the park headquarters in St. Croix Falls, but I said we wanted to work with the Stillwater Police. She said the Washington County sheriff's office is in Stillwater, too."

"Anything new on the missing couple?"

"She hasn't heard a word, and that's part of the problem. She's afraid the other agencies aren't keeping her informed on their investigations."

"It's tough to be out of the information loop, but if nothing is happening, there's nothing to tell her. Did she say any more about her personnel issue?"

"I asked, but she reiterated that she wouldn't get into it over the phone."

I heard the pre-boarding announcement and picked up my carryon bag.

Jill looked at her boarding pass. "We're in zone three."

I nodded toward the desk. "The airline will want us to pre-board. They don't like the other passengers bumping into cops' guns as they jostle through the boarding process. It raises issues."

Jill followed me to the boarding lane, and I flipped open my National Park Service credentials. "We're armed federal officers."

The attendant glanced at my credentials and boarding pass. "Have a nice flight."

Jill was right behind me as we entered the plane, and I identified myself to the lead flight attendant. She smiled and nodded. "We'll move you up if there are any open seats."

We put our bags into the overhead bins and sat down. Jill leaned close. "I like this service."

"They expect repayment if they have an unruly passenger."

Updrafts and turbulence made for a rough flight, and the seatbelt light stayed on most of the time. Aside from that, the flight was uneventful. We got our rental car and drove east through St. Paul on I-94.

"This is where you grew up?"

"Home was a few miles north of here, in Roseville."

"So, all this looks familiar?"

"It's changing all the time. Lots of it looks the same, but the stores and restaurants have turned over. The police station used to be right here, across from the National Guard Armory. It's moved out of downtown and I'll bet I don't know a single uniform cop in St. Paul anymore."

Within twenty minutes, we were driving toward Wisconsin and passing fields of corn. I took a back road into Stillwater to avoid the downtown traffic and pulled up in front of the stately inn suggested by Mark Guertin.

Jill stood next to me as I took our luggage out of the trunk. "This looks like an antebellum southern mansion."

We checked in, went to our room, and hung up our clothes. Jill looked out of the window.

"Is that the St. Croix River? It's only like two blocks away."

I nodded as I dialed Sandy Prudhomme's phone.

"Detective Prudhomme, this is Doug Fletcher from the National Park Service. We just flew in from Texas and checked into the

Stillwater Inn on Second Street. Can you meet us for lunch somewhere in Stillwater?"

"Mark Guertin said you were going to call. If you can give me half an hour, I'll meet you at The Dock restaurant. It's quiet, and I can show you the little bit we've got."

I stopped at the front desk and got directions to The Dock. We meandered along the river until we got to the restaurant where we got a table in the farthest room, overlooking the river and the loading wharf for the paddle boats.

"This is such a quaint place. It seems strange, but I hardly see a house on the other side of the river."

"This is part of the National Scenic Riverway, and development is strictly limited to retain the natural feel of the river. As I remember it, you can canoe from St. Croix Falls to Stillwater and feel like you're in the wilderness even though you're less than a mile from civilization."

A middle-aged brunette sat down next to Jill. "And that's part of the problem. There are lots of secluded islets and backwaters where people can do nefarious things." She put out her hand. "I'm Sandy Prudhomme. I assume you're Jill and Doug."

I tried to be gentlemanly and stand, but Sandy gestured for me to sit. "Thanks for meeting with us."

Sandy waved at the waitress. "Have you ordered yet?"

Jill handed her a menu. "Not yet. We've just been enjoying the river view. Thanks for suggesting this place."

The waitress came and took our orders. As she walked away, Sandy said, "The food is as good as the view. It's my favorite spot for dinner with my husband." She paused to make sure no one was listening. "I hate to drag you down, but I've got nothing you probably don't already know. Boaters found the partially submerged canoe floating past the lift bridge. It was stenciled with the outfitter's logo and had a number. They pulled it to the marina and called the outfitter, who called us. He'd already been in touch with the National Park Service and Coast Guard Reserve, so they'd been on the lookout for the canoeists, but no one has seen anything."

I waited while the waitress delivered our beverages. "Do you have any idea where the canoe was abandoned?"

"Not really. All we know for sure is that the couple launched near Taylors Falls on Friday, and the canoe was recovered here the next day. I can do all kinds of speculation, but the reality is the canoe might've capsized almost as soon as they got in the water. Or they could've been close to their scheduled pickup point, which should've taken between five and six hours after they launched."

Jill stirred her Diet Coke with her straw as she thought. "How fast would a canoe drift?"

"If it weren't half-full of water and drifted down the middle of the channel, it probably would've been in Stillwater Friday evening. It was half-full of water, so that'd slow it down, and if it drifted down the shoreline, it could've been caught in snags, fallen trees, bulrushes, or just slowly drifting down a side channel. Hell, we've had some rain, and it might've been hung up somewhere until the water level went up after the rain stopped."

Sandy leaned back and watched one of the paddle wheelers pull away from the dock, turn, and start upriver. "Bottom line is that there's no way to know where they separated from the canoe. There's about fifteen miles of river between the launch and O'Brien State Park. I don't know how you'd be able to narrow down the point they capsized."

The waitress delivered our meals, and we started eating. Jill took a bite of halibut and closed her eyes. "I think I've died and gone to heaven. This is incredible." She smiled at me. "Beats the steak and burger options on our last two investigations."

Sandy was eating a portobello mushroom cap in a hamburger bun. "I read up on you two a little. I found CNN stories about a fall at Devils Tower and a body in western South Dakota from last winter. Is that steak and burger country?"

Jill nodded. "I practically had to kidnap the cooks to get a salad."

I steered the conversation back to the missing newlyweds. "There's been no sign of them or their gear?"

Sandy shook her head. "To be honest, I've been expecting a boater to report their bodies floating in the river."

"As I recall, life jackets have been mandatory in Minnesota since I was a scout. Even if they swamped the canoe, they'd still be able to float to shore and walk to a road or house."

"Doug, the law says there have to be enough life jackets for all the occupants of a boat. It doesn't say they have to wear them. If the life jackets weren't being worn, they could've floated most of the way to Iowa by now. The same with their wooden canoe paddles."

"Was there any evidence of foul play in the canoe?"

"It'd been drifting for two days with a foot of water inside it. If there had ever been any evidence in it, the water had washed it away long before it got here."

We ate in silence for a while, having run out of questions and ideas. Sandy's eyes lit up. "Mark Guertin told me to ask you about Mary, Mary, quite contrary."

I shook my head, but Jill's interest had been piqued. "Who's Mary, Mary?"

"I was trying to arrest a drunk hooker in a downtown St. Paul hotel. I got her outside and was putting cuffs on her when she started wailing and offering me 'favors' if I didn't arrest her. A limo pulled up to drop the mayor and his wife off for dinner, and Mary, the hooker, was sobbing and upping her offers of sexual favors in explicit detail. The mayor's wife thought it was hilarious and asked if I negotiated with all the hookers I arrested. The story got around, and suddenly she was Mary, Mary, quite contrary, and I was the rookie cop who got kidded by the mayor's wife."

Jill looked at Sandy. "I hired Doug out of retirement. That wasn't anywhere in his personnel file."

Sandy finished her mushroom burger and wiped her mouth. "Mark said you were a hell of a cop. He asked if you'd be willing to work for him in Stillwater."

"That's kind of him, but I'm happy with the National Park Service. Jill and I just celebrated our first wedding anniversary, and we're buying a house in Texas."

"He told me a story about you wading into a frozen pond to rescue a woman and her dog from a car that ran off the road. I guess they would've died if you'd stood by and waited for the fire department. He also said you coached an inner-city youth baseball team and bought them uniforms and equipment. Overall, I'd say that makes you a hell of a cop."

Jill sensed my discomfort with the conversation and squeezed my hand. "He's a pretty good husband, too."

Sandy handed the waitress a credit card. "Lunch is on the Stillwater PD. If you have any questions or need some assistance, call my cellphone."

I took out a business card and wrote Jill and my cellphone numbers on the back. "I appreciate your honest assessment of a crappy situation. If anything comes up, please call us."

Sandy signed the charge slip and stood up. "I've got to say you two are a surprise. I read the clippings, and I expected two hardcore cops. Having lunch with you has been delightful, and I felt as at ease as I do with my siblings. If you get time some evening, there's a little wine bar up on Second Street that's a little noisy, but the food is good, and the wine selection is great. We could meet and swap war stories when we're off duty and able to have a glass of wine or two."

We shook hands and walked out together, promising to call if the case allowed. Jill and I walked back to the Inn.

Jill was subdued. "It sounds like the case is dead unless a body floats up."

We watched the lift bridge go up to let a sailboat and large cabin cruiser pass, going upstream. "We need to talk to the National Park Service and Coast Guard people who are on the water. Maybe they've got some perspective that Sandy wouldn't have as a detective."

"I told the superintendent we'd call as soon as we got checked in. How long will it take to drive to the park headquarters?"

We continued our walk back to the Inn past the shops and pubs in downtown Stillwater while I considered the question. "It's like fifteen miles on the water. I suppose it's half an hour driving."

"Didn't you grow up here?"

"St. Paul was home, and I was a passenger when Mom drove to Stillwater and Taylors Falls, but I've never driven it myself. I looked at the map and found a state highway going straight north, but it appears to be two lanes and goes through a few little towns."

Jill called Cheryl Britton while I packed water, sunscreen, and insect repellent we'd bought walking back to the inn.

"Cheryl will hang around the headquarters building until we get there. She said it's quickest to drive up the Minnesota side of the river and cross over the river at Taylors Falls. They're actually across the river, in Wisconsin."

Jill watched out the passenger side window. "I haven't seen the river since we left Stillwater," she said as we passed through Copas, a tiny town halfway to our destination.

"That's part of the St. Croix's attraction as a scenic river that needed protection."

"That also means there wasn't someone looking out their living room window who might've seen the canoeists."

"The only people who might've seen them were in boats or canoes on the water."

Chapter Four

Tuesday afternoon

We crossed the Taylors Falls bridge, parked the rental car, and then went inside the park headquarters and asked directions to the superintendent's office. Cheryl Britton appeared fortyish, with hair that was more salt than pepper. She looked up when we walked in, the stress and tiredness visible on her face.

"Can I help you?" she asked because we were dressed in civilian clothes, although we wore badges and holsters on our belts.

"I'm Jill Fletcher, and this is Doug Fletcher."

The weariness left Cheryl's face, and she smiled. "You have no idea how happy I am to see you."

She stepped from behind her desk and shook our hands. After directing us to guest chairs, she closed the office door.

I pulled my chair close to the desk. "Let's discuss your issues."

Cheryl closed her eyes. "Issues hardly describes what's going on. If you two can't help, I'm going to tear out my hair."

"Where would you like to start?" Jill asked.

"Finding the missing honeymoon couple. They rented canoes Friday, pushed off, and haven't been seen since."

"Don't the outfitters usually send renters out in groups?" I asked.

"The weekends are a zoo for them, so yes, they send out groups. But this couple went out on a quiet Friday morning, so it was just the two of them. They told the outfitter they were on their honeymoon."

"Isn't that risky?" Jill asked.

"Not usually. In the spring, the river can be kind of wild when the snowmelt comes along, especially through the narrow area in the dells, but by July, the river is down and placid. It's an easy paddle without rapids or many challenges. The biggest risk is taking a side channel when you get out of the dells."

Jill cocked her head. "What are the dells?"

"The first part of the river is bordered by the steep rock walls you probably noticed when you crossed over the bridge. On the weekends, there are lots of people walking and climbing the rocks. As a matter of fact, the rock climbers are our biggest source of rescues and first aid calls. Anyway, once you get past the rock walls, the shoreline drops off after the dells, and there are islands and side channels. The river current is almost unnoticeable unless you pull your paddles and just drift." Cheryl paused. "Matt said you've both been in canoes before."

I nodded. "I've done Boundary Waters canoe trips, and I've gone down the Namekagon River as far as the St. Croix with the scouts. That said, I haven't been in a canoe for thirty years."

"I've only canoed on lakes in the Ozarks when I was stationed there twenty years ago," Jill said.

Cheryl smiled. "Doug probably qualifies as intermediate, and Jill, you're a novice." Cheryl paused. "You're the most experienced of the investigative resources who were offered up. A day on the river with a couple of my rangers, and you'll both be pros."

"I appreciate your skills assessment, but I think it'd take more than a day to get us to the level of professional," Jill said.

"Have either of you ever fallen out of a canoe?"

"That was part of a canoeing merit badge. We had to swamp a canoe and get back into it."

Jill shook her head. "In my case, we just had a pleasant paddle along the shoreline without any upsets."

"Your biggest challenge will be getting back into shape. You'll be using muscles you've forgotten about."

"What have you done to investigate the disappearance?" I asked.

"The outfitter and I each sent out a canoe at sunset when the honeymooners didn't arrive at the pickup location. The outfitter's people checked the Minnesota shoreline, and my

41

people checked the Wisconsin side, which involves paddling the smaller channel. We also notified the Coast Guard and sheriff's water patrols. They checked the lower river, closer to Stillwater."

"They didn't find anything?" I asked.

"Nothing Friday night, but they were moving fast, looking for two people waving their arms and waiting to be rescued from shore or an island.

"Saturday morning, I sent out two canoes, and the outfitter asked the groups he sent out to watch for the missing pair. I also called the two scout camps and Dunrovin, the Catholic retreat, and asked them if they'd had anyone walk in. Saturday afternoon, I called again and asked them to check their shoreline…"

"Did anyone find anything other than the canoe that showed up in Stillwater?" Jill asked.

"The Coast Guard Reserve found a life jacket with the outfitter's logo."

I pointed to a map of the St. Croix River on Cheryl's wall. "Show me where the life jacket was found."

Cheryl studied the map for a second, then put her finger on an island where the St. Croix splits into the main channel on the Minnesota half of the river and a smaller channel on the Wisconsin side.

"The life jacket was found here, tangled in branches of an overhanging tree. We assumed it fell out of their canoe, but the outfitter said they lose a couple life jackets and paddles a year, and they're not numbered. So, we can't say for sure the honeymoon couple lost it."

Cheryl took a deep breath and blew it out. "I don't want to seem…" She tilted her head back and looked at the ceiling. "I wasn't ready to admit that my niece was anything more than stranded on the shore or an island somewhere. I'm still hopeful that they're lost, hiking through some area along the river, trying to find a house they can call from."

I put on my least threatening persona. "Tell me about them."

"What do you want to know?"

"How old are they? Are they experienced canoeists? Where are they from? Who's checking with their friends and family? Who's checking with the houses and farms along the river?"

"Whew! Let me get started and see how many questions I remember. They're in their early twenties. They graduated from college in May and got married last week. He's from Apple Valley, and she's from Edina. They met at Macalester College and fell in love. They've both been in canoes before, but this was their first time on moving water, and neither was more than novice status. That's not usually a problem this time of year. We have lots of novice groups who do fine. I've spoken with Washington County on the Minnesota side and Polk County on the Wisconsin side. I've also spoken with the Stillwater Police and the FBI. They all claim that they're helping, but I don't know if any of them picked up the ball, which is why I asked for your help. I just don't think anyone is pursuing this."

I sat down. "Put us in a couple of canoes with experienced rangers and let us explore the backwaters around the little islands."

Cheryl nodded. "I can start you this afternoon…"

Jill looked out the window at the late afternoon sun. "I know you don't want to leave them out there another night if you can help it, but we just arrived from Texas, and I think it'd be more productive if we started first thing in the morning."

Cheryl looked resigned to Jill's comments. "Sure. I'll get Keith and Greg ready to go tomorrow morning. I'll have them pack up for a full day on the water." Cheryl made herself a note.

I waited for a moment, then said, "Tell us about your personnel issue."

"One of my young rangers borrowed a cellphone from one of his female co-workers. After he made his call, it appears he looked through her phone and found some…intimate videos of several other rangers. It appears he emailed them to himself, then posted them on an internet site that allows anonymous posts of ex-girlfriends."

Jill fell back in her chair like she'd been deflated. "I always dreaded something like that. Who's the male ranger?"

"We don't know who did it, or even if it was a male ranger. We know several rangers saw the videos, and we know who's in the pictures. Beyond that, nobody owns up to it. I've spoken with the women whose pictures were posted, and well, both have pictures on their phones, and both have loaned their phones to other rangers."

"How intimate are the pictures?" I asked.

Cheryl weighed her words. "I thought they were pornographic, but I may be an old prude. Personally, I can't imagine anyone allowing themselves to be photographed in those...situations, so it makes it hard for me to objectively question the parties involved. I hope that having Jill here, a step away from the personalities, would allow a more meaningful interrogation of the parties involved."

Jill glanced at me, apparently seeking guidance. "Give us the names of the parties you know are involved and the name of the website."

Cheryl wrote the names of the female rangers and the website on a piece of paper and handed it to Jill. "I suggest you not look at the pictures until after you've interviewed the women. I had a hard time looking them in the eye after seeing the content."

Jill accepted the note. "Are either of them around now?"

Cheryl thought for a moment. "Suzy is probably in the gift shop. I think Randi is leading a summer camp tour. She'll be back by five. Both will be around tomorrow."

I stood. "Why don't you bring Suzy in here and let Jill talk to her. You can show me around the headquarters building and introduce me to the rangers, so they know who I am."

Cheryl left, and I was going to follow, but Jill grabbed my hand. "I don't want to get into this. You talk to Suzy."

"Let's assume Cheryl has a reason why she wants you to speak with the involved parties. You're less threatening, you're a good interviewer, and you're female. I bet these women will open to you. Think about how well you did with that girl in Hulett. You got her to throw her boyfriend under the bus."

Cheryl showed up with a petite brunette, wearing a Smokey Bear hat. "Suzy Barth, this is Jill Fletcher. She works for the National Park Service in Texas. Her husband, Doug, and I are going to take a tour of the headquarters."

The architecture and layout of the headquarters and gift shop were a variation of the rustic theme used in virtually all National Park Service buildings. Cheryl led me to a bookcase. "We have the usual regional books, local and natural history. No surprises." A dozen people were looking through the souvenirs and books.

I pointed to a door. "Is there a spot where we can talk privately outside?"

"Sure." Cheryl led me off a concrete sidewalk down a trail. "It's quiet here."

"Tell me more about Suzy and Randi. Have they been with you a long time?"

"They're both seasonal rangers, and they've been here the last two summers. They're pleasant, upbeat, knowledgeable, and professional. They've never given me any reason not to trust or respect them, and I've never had a complaint about them from our guests or their co-workers."

"Do they live near the park?"

"They share an apartment in St. Croix Falls, about five miles from the park entrance."

"Do they host a lot of parties or socialize a lot with the other rangers?"

"What's a lot? Virtually all the young rangers socialize with each other, or they don't last more than one season. I'm not part of the clique of young rangers, so they don't invite me out for drinks or to their parties, so I'm not the best person to ask about their social lives."

"Are they heterosexual, LBGTQ, or some other flavor?"

Cheryl looked down the trail. "I'm not sure where they fall on the spectrum. Based on the videos I saw from the website, I'd guess they are closer than just being roommates, but I really don't know that for a fact. They may have been acting for the videographer."

"Who was the videographer?"

Cheryl looked shocked. "I don't know. I never thought to ask that question. I guess that's part of the value of having you here. I'm too close to this to be objective. I looked at the videos, and my mind froze. My first thought was, 'Why in hell would you let someone take a picture of you naked?' My second question was, 'Why would you store those pictures on your phone-camera?'"

I guessed Cheryl was close to my age, or maybe a few years younger. "It's a different world from the one we grew up in. Jill and I were talking about her growing up in rural South Dakota. Her viewpoint was that no adult she'd met growing up had ever engaged in sex and that every child in the school had been born after immaculate conception."

Cheryl nodded. "I think sex was more rampant than we were led to believe, but I have the impression that it's not anywhere near the taboo I was taught it to be in Catholic school."

"Let's see if Jill and Suzy are through."

Cheryl's office door was open, and Jill was writing notes. Cheryl closed the door. "Did Suzy share anything with you?"

Jill tapped the pen on the paper a couple of times before answering. "Yes, and no. Yes, she believes the videos were stolen off her phone. She gave me the names of two people who've borrowed her phone and doesn't believe either of them would poach pictures from her or post them on the internet. She thinks it was an ex-boyfriend who borrowed Randi's phone."

I glanced at Cheryl. "Did she mention who the videographer was?"

"She said there wasn't a videographer. She and Randi were drinking one night, and they set up a phone and took the video themselves. Suzy also has an ex-boyfriend, and she was going to use the video to taunt him. He apparently was into lesbian videos, and she thought it would be fun to show them to him and say, 'Look what you're missing.'"

"Do you believe her?" I asked.

Jill wrinkled her nose. "It didn't pass the smell test. I tried to dig deeper, but she shut down."

I looked at Cheryl. "Can you get Randi here before Suzy has a chance to synch their stories?"

Cheryl picked up her cellphone and called the person who coordinated tours, asking her to send Randi in as soon as she got back. After she hung up, she said, "I think it's too late to keep them from comparing their stories. I got pretty much the same story from both Suzy and Randi when I spoke with them, although it never occurred to me to ask who took the video." Cheryl stopped for a moment, reflecting on something. "The story about them setting up a cellphone to take the video isn't true. The camera angle changed during the filming. Someone was holding the camera and moving it around."

"I didn't think she was telling me the unvarnished truth." Jill looked at me. "Maybe you should talk with Randi."

"No, this is your baby. I think it's important that you interrogate both." I paused and had a thought. "Show her your badge before you start asking questions and tell her it's a federal crime to lie to a National Park Service investigator, the same as it is to lie to an FBI agent. That might get her attention."

"I hate to play that card upfront. It'll put her on the defensive."

"Okay. Use your judgment but keep that in your pocket if she's equivocating."

"What if she asks for a lawyer?"

"I don't think that's a problem. Any lawyer will tell her she has to answer questions if she's not incriminating herself. If she claims her fifth amendment right not to incriminate herself, we have a very different investigation."

Jill made some notes, then asked Cheryl to tell us about the upcoming VIP visit.

"I hardly want to think about it. The Secret Service called me with the regional superintendent on the line to inform me they wanted to bring the President's son and his school class here for a canoe trip. Apparently, they'd investigated other options for an adventure outing and determined this to be the easiest to control. They set the date and then sent people here for a week, checking out the route, the surroundings, vetting my staff and the outfitters, and planning for contingencies. It's a nightmare."

"I'd think Isle Royale National Park would be a better choice," I said. "It's isolated, and access can be totally controlled."

"I don't know what they considered, but I know they were looking for canoeing adventures. They considered the Boundary Waters Wilderness Area and determined it would be impossible because of the restrictions on motorized vehicles and the sheer size of the park. Here they can monitor most of the trip by motorized boat and have a helicopter overhead. The shorelines can all be patrolled, and virtually all the access points can be closed for the day. The Coast Guard patrols the river as an interstate waterway and can restrict water access just north of the last marina. There are few private access points north of there, and we can shut down access from the north and on the Namekagon River. Someone will be watching almost every foot of the shoreline, and we'll supply a flotilla of law enforcement people."

"It hardly sounds like an adventure," Jill said.

"Compared to having a Secret Service agent with you every second of the day and being locked up inside the White House, this might be quite a wilderness experience."

There was a knock on the door, and then an attractive blonde ranger stuck her head inside the room. "Anna said you wanted to see me?"

Cheryl got up and waved Randi Johnson into the office. "Randi, Jill and Doug Fletcher are National Park Service investigators. Jill would like to ask you about the leaked video."

Randi looked extremely uncomfortable. "Cheryl, let's forget about it. This is embarrassing. I really don't want to talk about it with anyone else."

I got up and pushed my chair toward her. "Humor us. We were sent from Texas to look into the missing couple. Cheryl asked if we'd look into this too, while we're here."

Jill stood and put out her hand. "Hi, Randi. Let's chase Cheryl and Doug out so the two of us can talk."

Cheryl and I walked outside to the secluded trail. She took out a pack of Nicorette gum and popped a piece into her mouth. "It's weeks like this that make me want to start smoking again."

"I hear you. I pulled myself out of a whiskey bottle, and there are days when a shot would taste awfully good."

"Do you attend AA meetings?"

"I went cold turkey about two years ago. I was feeling sorry for myself after a divorce and a career-ending injury, and booze had been an easy answer for too long. I packed a U-Haul trailer full of stuff in St. Paul and unloaded it in Flagstaff. I started riding a bike, avoided the bars, and hit the reset button on my life."

"I heard you met Jill in Flagstaff."

"I was working as a seasonal ranger, and she needed an investigator for a murder. I fit the bill, and she talked me into taking on a different, albeit familiar role. I discovered that I missed being a cop, and she liked having a cop on staff."

Cheryl tapped the ring finger of her left hand. "When did the ring happen?"

"We became confidants, then friends. It didn't take long for us to figure out that we were both lonely, and we quickly became best friends."

"Being the park superintendent is tough. You're everyone's boss, and you really can't afford to become anyone's buddy."

"It's lonely at the top. I don't see a ring on your finger."

"He got tired of moving and decided to stay in Mississippi when I got this posting. We're not divorced, but that'll be the inevitable end. One of us will meet someone, and that'll precipitate a permanent solution. In the meanwhile, I tell people we're separated, but the reality is that the separation is permanent." Cheryl paused, then looked at me. "My god, you are good. I haven't told that to anyone, and I only met you an hour ago, but you've got me spilling my life story."

I smiled. "Sometimes, all you need is a kindred spirit, and you can share your burden. And to be fair, you got my backstory out of me before you started unburdening yourself."

"You're from St. Paul?"

"Yup. I graduated from Ramsey High School and worked as a St. Paul cop for nearly twenty years. Like I said earlier, I've canoed the Namekagon and spent a lot of weekends camping at the scout camp across the river from Stillwater."

"The scout camp was a big beneficiary of the Scenic Waterways Act. The politicians allowed the scouts to retain ownership of the riverfront camp property with some restrictions on development within sight of the river. The land all around them had been subdivided, and there were some cabins and houses, but a lot of the land was being held by speculators. When the law was enacted, the National Park Service started acquiring the property by eminent domain. People saw the handwriting on the wall, and a lot of them decided they'd rather give their land to the scouts as a tax write-off instead of selling to the government. I've heard the scout camp gained a mile of riverfront through donations."

"I've climbed the bluffs along the camp and never got more than a quarter-mile up the river from the cabins. There were stories about old, haunted houses further up the river. I'm not sure if that's true, or if some wise old camp ranger spread them to keep the scouts from wandering too far away from their campsites."

"I don't know if it's true, but I'm sure the Secret Service will be able to answer that question. They've got people walking every inch of the riverfront."

I laughed. "I pity the poor rookie agents who pull that duty. Those bluffs are full of poison ivy."

"I see rangers and guests covered with poison ivy welts after exploring the islands and shoreline. I've had a few guests who went in search of a place to squat and relieve themselves only to develop a rash in places that tend to chafe."

"Yeah, I had a tent-mate who was allergic to poison ivy, and he somehow ended up with blisters inside his underwear every camping trip."

Jill appeared behind us on the trail. "What about the poison ivy?"

I could see the interviews had taken a toll on her. "There's poison ivy all over the river valley. Be careful when you get out of your canoe."

"I've never seen poison ivy. What's it look like?"

"There's an old scout adage, 'Leaves of three, let it be.'"

"A lot of it is low ground cover, usually in shaded places," Cheryl added. "But it also will climb like an ivy plant. I had a late fall group come through who'd been duck hunting off the national riverway. They'd gone out in the dark and constructed a duck hunting blind before sunrise. As it got light, they realized they'd made the blind out of poison ivy. They were covered with blisters on their arms and faces."

Jill grimaced. "I guess I'll avoid any three-leafed plants."

I bent down and pointed to a three-leafed plant alongside the trail. "These are wild strawberries. Poison ivy leaves are darker green, waxy, and have a coarser serrated margin. This time of year, they might have tiny white flowers."

Jill pulled out her cellphone and pulled up pictures of poison ivy plants. "Here it is. I should avoid this because I'll get an itchy rash."

I shook my head. "It's not an itchy rash. Think I-T-C-H-Y in capital letters, like losing sleep and going nuts. It causes blisters that can spread if you touch or scratch them. Untreated, the itching can last for two weeks."

Jill nodded and put her phone in her pocket. "Randi was interesting. She and Suzy had gotten their story together. She also suggested letting it go and stood up to leave. I made her sit down and tried to be sympathetic, but we couldn't connect. I finally resorted to Doug's suggestion of explaining that I was a federal officer."

"How did she react to that?" Cheryl asked.

"She stopped talking and stared at me. Then she asked why I was involved at all. I explained Cheryl's reporting to National Park Service Human Resources, and that the theft of the pictures and sharing them online was a federal crime. It took her a while to digest that. Then she stared at her shoes and said it was just a stupid thing."

"Did she open up after that?" I asked.

"Not at all. She stopped talking and sat there, staring at her shoes. After a minute of silence, she looked up and asked if she could leave. When I said no, she broke into tears. We sat there for almost five minutes, and then she said she didn't want to talk about it anymore. I told her that wasn't an option. I told her that her job was at risk if she didn't cooperate."

Cheryl stared off into the distance. "I wish I had a cigarette." She clenched her jaw. "Suzy and Randi are the victims, not the perpetrators."

"That's what I told her. I said we were there to help get to the bottom of what had happened and not to persecute or embarrass her. She stood up and said, 'It's too late for that.' She opened the door and walked out."

Cheryl looked at me. "Now what? I'm not going to fire Suzy and Randi because someone violated their privacy while in their off-park residence."

I mulled Jill's comments. "Something isn't right. I wonder if they're getting pressured by the thief or his cohorts. Their privacy has been severely compromised, and they're acting like it's no big thing, asking Jill to drop the investigation."

Cheryl spat her nicotine gum into the wrapper and took out another piece. "I don't know how to proceed. Doug, what do you do with rape victims who don't want to cooperate with an investigation?"

"I usually point out that they're the victims and show sympathy. I tell them that the rapists are predators, and if they don't help, it's going to allow the rapist to hurt more women." I thought about Randi and Suzy's situation. "This is different because it was more a crime of opportunity, unlike a rape that usually is a man showing his dominance over the victim."

Jill's eyes brightened. "Maybe that's it. Maybe it's the same. Whoever did this has diminished them, not physically but psychologically. They're cowering from their attacker. He's stripped them naked on the internet. Maybe he's got something more he's holding over them."

Cheryl started chewing her gum vigorously. "I suppose he may have more video that he hasn't released."

I looked at her. "We haven't seen the video. Do you think there might be something more provocative that wasn't posted?"

Cheryl blushed as she reflected on what she'd seen. "I have a hard time believing there could be anything more graphic than what I saw."

Jill looked between us. "I really don't want to see the video." She paused. "You said there were some rangers you suspected of accessing the video and posting it on the internet. Who were they?"

"I don't *know* who was involved, but I suspect it was one of two guys. Randi and Suzy each told me they'd loaned their phones to one ranger. I asked the two guys about borrowing the phones, without revealing that I knew about the video, just asking if they'd looked at personal information when the phones were in their possession. Both denied having done anything but make a call."

I was struck with a thought. "How did you find out about the video? Did Randi or Suzy report it being stolen from them?"

"No, Randi and Suzy were shocked when I asked them about the video. They initially denied everything. I assured them it was them in the recording, and then they became frantic."

When Cheryl paused, I waited for more, then said, "You didn't answer my question."

"One of the other young rangers, Laurel, took me aside and said her boyfriend was approached by one of his buddies, asking if he knew the park rangers in a porn video. He told the friend he doubted it, but they pulled up the website. The video is titled National Park Service Honeys. He recognized Suzy and warned Laurel about it. She came to me rather than embarrassing Randi and Suzy."

"That didn't work very well," Jill said.

"It took the burden off Laurel and dumped it on me."

"Do you think Laurel is involved?" I asked.

"I'm sure she never saw the video. As a matter of fact, I think she was disgusted that her boyfriend had watched it."

Jill looked at me for an opinion.

"It's not something that comes up in discussions with my friends. I suspect, and it's only a suspicion, that many young guys use the internet for perverse things. For example, the FBI was monitoring a whole bunch of websites offering 'services' because human trafficking groups use those to solicit customers."

Jill brightened. "Call Jess Pond and give him this website. Maybe his people can backtrack to the person who posted it."

Cheryl looked confused. "Who's Jess Pond?"

"He's the FBI Special Agent in Charge of the Rapid City office," I said. "He's been more than helpful in the past."

Jill struggled to stifle a yawn.

Cheryl looked at her watch. "It's after five. Most of my people are probably gone, and you two look like you're ready to drop. Let's call it a day, and I'll get you on the water tomorrow morning."

I took out a business card and wrote my cellphone number on the back of it. "If something comes up, you can call me any time."

* * *

I drove the Wisconsin side of the river back to Stillwater. Jill watched the farms, houses, and wooded plots go past. "It's hard to get my head around the fact that we're only half an hour away from a major metropolitan area with over three million people."

"A lot of the development grew southwest of Minneapolis, although the St. Paul side has crept a few miles east since I was a kid. The Wisconsin side of the river hasn't grown as much because there are only a few bridges across, and this area only had the two-lane Stillwater bridge as an access point until a couple years ago. It's starting to grow more now, but the housing still can't get close to the river because of the Scenic Waterways Act."

We crossed into Minnesota at Osceola and followed the highway into Stillwater. I parked at the ramp next to the Inn. "What would you like for supper?"

"Is there anything close?"

I laughed. "There are two restaurants in the Inn and another dozen within two blocks. You can have anything from fondue to Chinese within walking distance."

"How about somewhere I can get an interesting salad."

I spoke to the desk clerk, and he made a phone call while I waited. After the call, he wrote a short note and handed it to me.

"We've got reservations at the wine bar Sandy mentioned. Do you want to clean up, or shall we just walk over?"

"If I go up to the room and change, I might just go to bed." Jill looked at her jeans and shirt as a couple dressed in a suit and dress waited to be seated in the inn's dining room. "Will they take us like this?"

"I think you'll see clothing from shorts to sport coats at most of the places in Stillwater. You'll be fine."

Jill hooked my arm. "Let's go!"

Chapter Five

The wine bar was exactly that. There was a long bar, lined with people sitting on bar stools, and across from it, a row of tables ran along a set of tall windows. The entire café probably only seated forty people. A guy wearing a white apron and white shirt met us at the door. His outfit seemed out of place with his dark goatee and tattooed arms.

"Fletcher. The inn just called and made a reservation for us."

The man smiled. "I have a nice corner table for you. Would you like a glass of wine? We have an extensive wine list on the back of the menu, and the chalkboard has selections by the glass."

Jill scanned the chalkboard. "I'll have a Malbec."

The waiter looked at me. "Tonic and lime, please."

He left us with menus, and Jill looked out the windows. The street was mostly in shadows as the sun dropped closer to the horizon. "This place is trendy and nice. Too bad they don't have a river view like our lunch restaurant."

"This is probably the low rent district," I said, scanning the menu. "Although the prices don't reflect that."

Jill looked at the menu and smiled. "I love it. Look at all the creative choices, and all of them either are a salad or include one. Yum."

The waiter came back with our drinks in less time than it took to read the menu. Jill chose a salmon salad, and I ordered the London broil.

Jill sipped her wine and smiled. "Not having wine tonight?"

"I'd fall asleep walking back to the Inn."

The weekday evening crowd didn't fill the café, and the din from a dozen diners echoed off the tin ceiling. I leaned across the table, trying to keep my voice down. "What do you think about Suzy and Randi's stories?"

"I felt sorry for them. They'd been violated, and there I was, picking at the wound. How is this even our issue? The filming took place in their apartment. Shouldn't the local police be investigating it?"

"It's affecting their job performance and the park. If one of the rangers uses it to create a hostile workplace, that's a National Park Service problem, and it seems to be affecting the interaction of the rangers. If it drives Suzy and Randi away, Cheryl loses two experienced rangers. As you know, losing experienced and talented people leaves a hole that may be hard to fill."

Jill swirled her wine and took a sip. "Okay, so it's a workplace issue. I still feel horrible about questioning Suzy and Randi."

I put my hand on Jill's. "That's why Cheryl wanted you rather than me to talk with them. You're non-threatening and compassionate. They'd take one look at me and think 'cop' and be totally freaked out."

Jill looked around. "Your dinner will be a few minutes. Call Jess Pond from the parking lot and see if he's willing to put someone on tracing the source of the internet post."

I walked to the parking lot and dialed Jess' number. "Hi, Doug. What's up?"

"I'm sorry to bother you at home. I've got a problem, and you might have the resource to help me out."

Jess chuckled. "I'm not at home. Things are a little backed up here, and I'm sitting at my desk. What do you need?"

I explained the video, the history of its travel to the internet, and the tension it caused at the park. I took out the note from Cheryl and read the address to Jess. I heard keys clicking and a pause.

"Oh shit. This is some serious pornography. I'm sure there's an alarm going off on the FBI server because I accessed this site." He paused. "What did you think of it?"

"I haven't looked at it, and I don't intend to. Judging by your reaction, I assume it's something that would be disruptive if the subjects' co-workers watched it."

"Co-workers, parents, and neighbors would all probably have a problem with it. Hell, if they filmed this in an apartment, they might lose their lease. Worse yet, we've had unscrupulous landlords try to extract payment in kind. What do you want?"

"Can your guys find out who posted this?"

"They can try, but most people that post crap like this are smart enough to cover their internet tracks. I'll pass it to my internet expert and see what he can find."

"Thanks. How are things going?"

"It's hotter than hell. Sturgis bike week is coming, and we're trying to help the locals keep a lid on things. Then there's the usual stuff. Between those things and the bureaucratic paperwork, I'm keeping busy. Are you in Texas?"

"Jill and I are on a temporary assignment in Minnesota. There's a missing couple who were canoeing on the St. Croix River, and we were asked to look into it."

"What's that got to do with the porn you just sent me?"

"That popped up as a sidelight to the missing people."

"Isn't the St. Croix the dividing line between Wisconsin and Minnesota?"

"Yes."

I heard computer keys clicking. "The Minneapolis FBI office has an agent assigned to that because of the interstate aspect. You should give her a call."

"Jess, you know how I feel about the FBI. You're the one person in the bureau I respect."

"The assigned agent is Margaret Steller. Maggie's been around the block a couple times, and I don't think she'll burn you. Call her."

"I haven't heard her name associated with the investigation."

Jess laughed. "That should tell you a lot. She's not in the bureau for the glory. She's a team player and often works best in the shadows."

"Jill's waving at me from the restaurant. Thanks for taking a crack at the trace. I'll give Special Agent Steller a call after we get off the water tomorrow."

"Off the water?"

"We're canoeing down the river to look at the areas where the couple might've disappeared."

"Bring your sunscreen."

"Got it and insect repellent."

My salad and London broil were on the table. Jill had switched to white wine, so I knew she was on at least her second glass. Our waiter was leaning on the table, having an earnest discussion with Jill. He stood up and put out his hand.

"I apologize. I thought you guys were probably local cops. We don't get many feds in here. I'm Rusty, the owner."

I shook his hand and introduced myself. "I should probably dive into my meat before it gets any colder."

"I've got a Cabernet that's great with the London broil. Can I get you a glass?"

I sat down. "Thanks, but I'm the designated driver tonight."

"I saw you walk over from the Inn." Rusty nodded his respect for my choice not to drink. "I'll get you another tonic and lime."

I pushed my salad aside and dove into the London broil.

"What did Jess say?"

"He pulled up the website and said it would probably set off alarms on the FBI server."

"Serious pornography."

"I think so. He's going to have his people look for the source, but it's unlikely they'll find anything. He gave me the name of the Minneapolis FBI agent who's assigned to the case of the missing St. Croix canoeists."

Jill knew my checkered past with the FBI and looked worried.

"Jess said she's a good head who likes to work from the shadows. I promised to call her when we got off the river."

Rusty delivered my tonic. "Everything good here?"

Jill speared the last piece of salmon. "This is wonderful. What do you use for the marinade?"

"Secret family recipe." Rusty smiled. "Soy sauce, lime juice, and crushed garlic. How's the London broil?"

"Tasty and done perfectly."

"Great. I hope you saved room for dessert. A couple of them are award winners."

Jill groaned. "Can I come back for a midnight snack?"

"Knock on the door if I lock up early."

"He's good," Jill said as Rusty walked away.

"That and great food keep people coming back."

Jill pushed her bowl away. "It's only seven o'clock, and I feel like it's bedtime."

"Mandy delivered us to the airport at three this morning. I think you can be forgiven for going to bed before the sun sets."

We took a leisurely walk through a few Stillwater downtown blocks, getting strange looks from people who noticed our pistols. I was asleep before the eight o'clock television shows came on. I woke up at midnight, went to the bathroom, and turned off the television.

Chapter Six

Wednesday

Cheryl was in her office when we arrived at 7:30. She handed each of us a rubberized backpack. "There are gloves, water bottles, granola bars, sunscreen, and insect repellent in the bags. Tie the bags into your canoes. Greg and Keith are down at the launch with canoes and paddles."

I turned off my cellphone and put it into the dry bag, then took out a bottle of sunscreen. Both of us wore quick-drying nylon pants and UPF rated long-sleeved shirts. Experience told me any exposed skin would be fried by the time we got off the river, so I slathered sunscreen on my face, neck, and hands.

"How long will we be on the river?" Jill asked, accepting the sunscreen from me.

"It's a five-hour trip from here to O'Brien State Park if you stay in the current and don't dawdle."

I sprayed insect repellent on my Minnesota Twins cap, neck, arms, and legs. "And if we explore the backwaters?"

"It'll take you days to explore all the little channels, inlets, swamps, and islets."

Jill took the insect repellent. "Has anyone done that yet?"

Cheryl looked down. "No. We've been working under the assumption they're alive and would be awaiting pick up."

I could see that Cheryl wasn't prepared to have this move from rescue to recovery. "We need to do that. As you said, it'd take Jill and me days to check all the little backwaters. Do you have more resources you could put into this?"

"Um, sure. I can move some people around to cover things. Probably not today, but by tomorrow, I could put out two or three more canoes with rangers. I'll pull in a couple of the people I've got on the Namekagon."

Jill put one hip on Cheryl's desk and looked down at her. "I'm sorry. We might find them somewhere, but this is the time to start exploring every possibility."

Cheryl took a deep breath and blew it out. Her eyes had tears. "At some level, I know what you're saying. The Aunt Cheryl in me is just unwilling to accept the…"

I closed the office door, and Jill knelt next to Cheryl as she cried. "Hey, there's a glimmer of hope. Don't give up totally."

Cheryl opened a drawer and pulled out a tissue. "Thanks...for being here. You're the right people, and you've got your heads on right." She sniffled, wiped her nose, and threw the tissue in the wastebasket. "Don't skimp on the insect repellent if you're going to poke around the backwaters. The mosquitoes will suck you dry."

Jill got up. "I've been in lots of parks with mosquitoes."

"You're going into their breeding ground. If you've never seen Minnesota mosquitoes, you're in for a treat. I swear that each of them can suck out one cc of blood. And we're warning people about them carrying equine encephalitis, so it's not just the miserable itching, there's also a bona fide health risk."

I opened the door and pulled the dry pack over my shoulder. "We'll also have to watch for poison ivy if we get out of the canoes and start poking around on land."

"This just keeps getting better and better," Jill said as Cheryl led us out of the headquarters building and took us to the canoe launch.

* * *

Greg and Keith sat on a wooden railing, waiting for us. There were two scarred aluminum canoes on shore with a dry bag strapped into the center of each. Our guides were young, lean, tanned, and handsome. They both wore National Park Service t-shirts, shorts, and floppy hats that almost matched Jill's hat.

Greg shook our hands, handed me a life jacket, then looked at the Sig on my belt. "Are you afraid of getting your gun wet?"

Jill laughed. "He got knocked out of a boat in a Padre Island backwater. A little oil and it was as good as new."

Greg looked like he'd just been saddled with a forty-something rookie. "You fell out of a boat."

"We were almost swamped when a boat's wake hit us. I was shooting at the boater with a shotgun, and my priority was making sure the shotgun stayed in the boat."

Greg looked impressed by my explanation. "I hope you won't need the gun here."

I put on the life jacket and zipped it. "I hope that every time I hook it to my belt."

Keith took Jill's dry bag as she put on her life jacket. "The problem is, you don't need a weapon until you need it immediately and badly," Jill said.

Greg thought about that for a moment. "I've never run across a situation where I felt I needed protection." Then he led me to the right hand canoe.

"Last year, there were more rangers injured by visitors than by animals, lightning, and falls combined."

Cheryl walked us to the edge of the river. "That's really a sad statistic."

Keith helped Jill into the front of the canoe and pushed them off. I hesitated for a second, looking back at Cheryl. "Hang in there. We're here to help, not make your life miserable."

Greg gave me a funny look. "What's that mean?"

I got into the front of the canoe without tipping it and picked up the paddle. I'd been dreading the transition into the canoe, not wanting to look like a rookie or idiot who'd lied about his level of expertise. "The search has probably gone from rescue to recovery."

Greg pushed us off and deftly turned the canoe with the current. "You think the people are dead?"

I spoke over my shoulder as I took easy strokes, using my back rather than my arms. "After four days without any sign of them, I'd say it's likely. What's the longest you've ever had a canoe missing?"

"It's only happened a couple times, and we found the missing people before dark."

"That's exactly why I'm concerned. If they were uninjured and onshore, they'd be waving at every passing canoe. Even if only one got injured, the other would be waving to get someone's attention."

"I suppose."

"I heard someone found one of the missing life jackets."

Greg adjusted our direction as we got into the swift current rushing down the dells. I slowly paddled while he steered us around small rapids and ripples, hinting at rocks below the surface. Jill and Keith were a hundred yards ahead of us doing the same.

"We're not sure the life jacket was from them," Greg said when he could concentrate on the question instead of the river. "It had the outfitter's logo stenciled on it, but they've had other canoes come back missing a life jacket. People get out of the dells, and they don't feel threatened by the water anymore, so they take the jackets off and throw them into the canoes. They get blown out by the wind or get knocked out by the paddles."

* * *

It took an hour to reach the area where the rocky walls turned to grassy hills, and the current slowed. We passed a boat launching ramp on the Minnesota side of the river. Keith and Jill pulled alongside us as we drifted slowly.

The bustle of the nearby Twin Cities had vanished, replaced by chirping birds and trilling cicada. Greg stopped paddling. "Ahead are some of the first side channels and islands. It'll be quicker if we split up. Doug and I can take the Wisconsin side and go past the campgrounds on Peaslee and Lower Lakes if you guys take the Minnesota side. We'll meet you somewhere past Osceola when you come out of the islands."

Jill and Keith nodded their agreement, so we paddled to the left and were soon going through a narrow channel. "What are the chances our missing people took this channel?"

"I'd say the odds are against this as being their route. It doesn't look like the main channel, and they'd have to be in search of an adventure to go this way."

The light breeze we'd felt in the main channel disappeared and mosquitoes hovered over us. None were biting, but I thought about Cheryl's comments on getting sucked dry by the insects. It made me wonder how well the lost couple had prepared for the sun and bugs.

We'd paddled for a while when a creek appeared, and Greg steered us toward the opening. "This is Peaslee Lake. I can't imagine how they would've thought this would be an option, but you wanted to check everywhere, right?"

"Right."

There was an empty campground as soon as we turned. "Let's put in here and look around."

The canoe scraped, and I stepped out, trying to look like I knew what I was doing. The campground was nothing more than a grassy opening. I walked the edges of the grass, looking for anything suspicious while Greg watched from the middle of the opening.

"Nothing?" he asked.

"The grass is matted. Do these campgrounds get a lot of use?"

We got back into the canoe. "They're sometimes busy on the weekends but not as much during the week."

My twisted thoughts ran to a dark place, imagining this as a perfect place to ambush someone without a witness anywhere in sight. "Do you ever have any problems back here?"

"What kind of problems?"

"Assaults? Robberies? Thefts?"

"I can't remember anyone ever having a problem in the rustic campgrounds." Greg paused. "If there's ever a problem, it's somewhere more accessible. I guess the bad guys don't like to exert this much effort to steal stuff."

I thought about the comments the rangers at Wind Cave National Park made about campers and hikers being a friendly bunch of people. My perspective was that they were an unsuspecting pool of potential victims. They were right more often than I was. We'd been investigating a murder, which made me right at least once.

Peaslee Lake was oversold. It didn't take us ten minutes to paddle the shoreline and determine there wasn't any evidence that anyone had been out of a canoe there recently. We went past the campground and back into the side channel, which took us a different route than the one we'd taken in. We came to another campground as the channel widened in Lower Lake. There was a canoe onshore and a green tent pitched on the edge of the clearing. A small column of smoke climbed lazily toward the sky.

Greg nosed our canoe next to the other one, and I got out. Two teenaged men were poking at a campfire. They seemed annoyed that we'd intruded on their serenity. I caught a whiff of marijuana smoke mixed with the wood smoke. One of the teens spotted my pistol, and his eyes went wide. He flipped the last of his joint into the smoldering campfire and stood.

"What's up?"

I chose to ignore the marijuana. "How many days have you guys been camping here?"

"We paddled down yesterday and spent the night."

"We lost a couple on Friday. You haven't had anyone wander around looking for assistance?"

The second teen got up. He was shirtless and had a couple of tattoos on his arms. "You're the only people we've seen since we got on the river." He glanced at my pistol. "What kind of cop are you?"

"National Park Service."

The teens looked at each other. "The National Park Service has cops?"

I nodded. "If you see the missing man and woman, or if you see something suspicious, please report it when you get off the river."

"Uh, sure. No problem."

Greg pushed us toward the lake. "You didn't hassle them about the dope."

"We've got bigger issues than a couple kids smoking dope in a secluded campsite. Don't you agree?"

"I don't bug people about marijuana unless they're making trouble or camping next to a family with kids. Most of them are mellow and not looking for trouble. I'm surprised you're not hassling them. You're a cop. Didn't you take a Hippocratic oath or something?"

I laughed. "I took an oath, but as you said, if they're not bugging anyone, I'm not going to get into it with them. Besides, I forgot my pen and citation pad in Texas."

Greg and I had a long talk about life in Texas and some of the other places I'd been as we meandered around Lower Lake. The time went by quickly, and we were back in the main channel, going downriver.

"There's a channel on the Minnesota side here."

"That's where Keith and your partner went. There's a bunch of little islands in there, but it's probably quicker to check them than our trip through the lakes was. They're probably waiting for us past Osceola."

We passed under the highway bridge at Osceola, and as predicted, Keith and Jill were drifting along ahead of us. We paddled up to them and drifted alongside.

"We saw nothing but a couple kids smoking weed in a remote campground. How about you guys?"

Jill looked totally relaxed. "Lots of mosquitoes and nothing else."

Keith reached across and grabbed our canoe. "I've got PBJs and a couple cans of Coke. You guys ready to eat here?"

He handed out peanut butter and jelly sandwiches and Coke. It brought back images of long-forgotten camping and canoe trips with friends long gone to adulthood and family members who'd moved to the corners of the country.

Jill noticed that I'd checked out. "What're you thinking about?"

"Scouts I knew way back when. Mike and Mark, Bob, and Dennis. I was just daydreaming and wondering where they are now."

"They're probably cooped up in some stuffy office, slaving away to make a buck."

Keith snorted his Coke. After sputtering and choking, he finally wiped his eyes. "You mean unlike us who are out here living the good life but unable to afford rent, a reliable car, and food on our massive ranger salaries. Yup, this is heaven."

I handed him the plastic bag my sandwich had been wrapped in and drained my Coke. "What next?"

"All the next islands and backwaters are on the Minnesota side. Jill and Keith can take the side channel. Doug and I will explore the backwaters off the main channel."

The day wound on with us switching sides of the river, swatting mosquitoes, reapplying sunscreen, and making one bathroom stop at a tiny campground. It was mid-afternoon, and tedium started to set in along with the aching of forgotten and unused muscles.

"Doug, that's the Soo Line bridge ahead. The channel splits just past the bridge. You and I can take the left, and when we meet up, we'll call it a day. That'll leave about the same amount of river to cover tomorrow."

"Sounds like a plan to me."

We shared the plan with Jill and Keith, then Greg pulled a cellphone out of his pack and called someone, requesting a pickup at Log House Landing.

The channel we chose was smaller than the main river channel but big enough for the current to carry us along. The shoreline was littered with limbs and stumps that had washed down when the water was higher. The left side was steep, and the right was a large island likely to be submerged during the annual spring floods. There was no evidence anyone had been through, and I was daydreaming when something flashed and caught my eye.

"On the right." I dug the blade of my paddle in on the left side of the canoe, pushing us toward the island.

"It's a bobber, hanging from a limb," Greg said from the back.

"Let's get closer."

As Greg said, a red and white bobber dangled from a limb. A chrome-plated swivel sparkled in the sunlight as it twisted. There was no wind, and the twisting of the swivel made me curious. "Let's go right up to it."

"Be careful. There's probably a branch under the water, and it may tip us."

The submerged branches were small and didn't cause any problems. Greg pushed the bow of the canoe into the tree so I could reach the bobber. The clear, monofilament fishing line went into the water at an angle, and when I pulled on it, there was resistance.

"It's probably caught in the branches, Doug."

Whatever it was attached to was heavy but moved as I pulled. I untangled the broken segment of line from the tree and pulled on the line.

Greg chuckled. "If there's a sturgeon or big catfish hooked on the other end of that line, let go before it tips us over."

"It's dead weight. I think a fish would tug a little."

"Not the big guys. They just lie on the bottom until you try to lift them, then they take off like a dragster."

We drifted until the line was going straight down.

"Hold us here while I pull on this."

"Doug, don't lean over the gunwale, or we'll be swimming when that line breaks."

I pulled and felt something heavy gradually rise from the bottom. I thought of Greg's warning about a big catfish taking off, so I was prepared for that or the line breaking. It was a heavy fishing line, meant to catch something hefty, so it allowed me to continue pulling.

"How deep is it here?"

"I don't imagine it gets over four or five feet, but I don't really know."

The item on the bottom came up slowly. I had three feet of line in the canoe when I leaned over the gunwale to peek in the water. Something light-colored was below me, but it wasn't discernable.

"You might as well give up. It's probably just a tire or dead branch."

I kept pulling, peeking carefully without tipping the canoe. With four feet of line in the canoe, I saw a wristwatch.

"We've got a problem."

"Just let go," Greg said, sounding irritated.

I shook my head. "There's a wristwatch down there, and it looks like it's attached to an arm."

I felt the canoe shudder as Greg shifted, attempting to look into the water. "Holy…What are we going to do?"

"What are the chances we'll be able to get a dead body into the canoe?"

"Slim and none."

"Look at the landmarks and make a mental note of where we are. I'm going to let go of the fishing line and hope the bobber stays attached. We're coming back with the Coast Guard or sheriff's department, and we need to locate this exact spot again."

I let the fish line slide slowly through my fingers, hoping it would stop before we reached the bobber. There were at least two feet of line left when I threw the bobber into the water. I looked around, noting the downed tree where the bobber had been hung up—a rock, a stump, and a clump of bulrushes.

"Do we have cell service here?"

"Probably."

I took my cellphone out of the dry bag and started to dial 911, then went to recent calls and found Sandy Prudhomme's cellphone number.

"Fletcher?"

"Hi, Sandy. I've got a problem. I've found a body in the river."

"Who've you called?"

"You."

"Where are you?"

"We're in a backchannel south of the Soo Line bridge."

"Wisconsin or Minnesota side?"

"Does it make a difference?"

Sandy let out a sigh. "Yeah. Maybe not. Well, not right now. I'll call the Coast Guard, and we'll let them sort out which county coroner to call."

I looked around and realized we'd drifted fifty yards downstream from the bobber. "What do you want me to do?"

"Stay there. I'll contact the dispatcher, and we'll figure out what to do. I'll call you back."

Chapter Seven

Jill and Keith were waiting for us when we paddled out of the backchannel. My face must've betrayed my intensity because Jill tensed as we approached. "What did you find?"

"There's a sunken body."

"Is it one of the missing honeymooners?"

We paddled alongside, and Keith grabbed our gunwale to keep the canoes together. Greg looked ill. "We didn't get him out of the water. Doug just pulled him up far enough to determine it was a human at the end of the line."

"End of the line?" Jill asked.

"I found a fishing bobber hooked on a tree. When I pulled in the line, there was a body hooked at the end. I called Sandy Prudhomme, and she's going to contact the Coast Guard. She asked us to stay here until she calls back or the Coast Guard boat arrives."

Jill's jaw twitched. I could tell she had a hundred questions. "Why didn't you pull the body out?"

"There's no way to pull a dead body into a canoe, and I was afraid we'd break the line if we tried to drag him to shore."

"You're sure it was a *him*?"

"All I could see was the wrist and a large, men's watch. I let it drop back to the bottom with the fishing line and bobber still attached."

Jill frowned. "I thought dead bodies floated?"

"They do after a few days in the water. The bacteria start producing gas almost the second you die. Bodies are usually buoyant after three or four days this time of year."

"It's been five days since the honeymoon couple disappeared."

"The gas production isn't an exact science." I paused. "Then, there may be other factors. It may not be our missing person; the guy may not have died the day they disappeared, or his body may be weighed down."

"There are a lot of snags on the bottom," Greg said. "Fishermen are always losing gear on dead trees and stuff. The body may just be tangled in stuff on the river bottom."

"I suppose that's the deal with the bobber. I suppose some fisherman snagged the body and broke his line when he attempted to pull it in."

Jill looked at the island behind us. "I suppose we should walk the island to see if there's any evidence."

Keith shuddered. "I don't think so. That whole island is a thicket covered in poison ivy."

I looked over my shoulder. "Do you know if that's in Wisconsin or Minnesota?"

"I'm not sure," Keith replied. "If I had to guess, I'd say it's in Wisconsin. The line between the states mostly splits down the main channel of the river. The little boat launch we went past is Wisconsin. What difference does it make?"

"The responsibility for investigating the death lies with the county where the body is recovered. I'm inclined to let the county sheriff's department search the island for evidence."

Keith smiled. "I like that plan. I don't want to deal with the poison ivy, mosquitoes, or deer ticks."

My phone trilled. By the time I got it out of the bag, the call had rolled over to voicemail. I checked the call log before the voicemail logo popped up and dialed Sandy Prudhomme.

"Hey, Doug, I was just leaving you a message. The Coast Guard is down by Bayport. They're motoring north, but there may be a Polk County boat that can get to you first. Will you need divers to recover the body?"

"He's on the bottom in about six feet of water, so yes, we probably need divers. We've got the body marked, so they won't have to search to find him."

"Could you tell if it was the guy you were searching for?"

"All I saw was a hand and a wristwatch. At that point, we knew we couldn't recover the body from a canoe, so we marked the spot and moved to the main channel."

"Have you called the FBI yet?" When I didn't immediately respond, she went on. "It's an interstate crime, and they have jurisdiction."

"I know, but my interactions with them haven't always been...positive. I talked to the special agent in charge of the Rapid City office, and he suggested I call Margaret Steller. Have you dealt with her?"

"That's not a name I know. If you got her name from someone you trust, it'd be a place to start. You've got plenty of time. I don't think anyone's going to respond to your location for close to an hour."

I ended the call. "It's going to be an hour before anyone gets here."

We watched a group of people pass in three canoes. They were young, none of them wore life vests, and they appeared to be enjoying some beers. They waved and hooted at us. "Let's paddle over to the little boat launch on the channel instead of fighting the current to stay here."

Wc paddled around the south end of the island into the narrow side channel where we'd found the body. The boat launch was little more than a gravel path down to the water with a few parking spots. We pulled the canoes onto the shore.

Jill grimaced. "What is that smell?"

Keith nodded toward a fifty-five-gallon drum near the parking lot. "I imagine someone cleaned their fish here and dumped the entrails into the drum."

The look on Jill's face said she wanted me to make sure the smell wasn't the other honeymooner. "It's not the smell of human decay. It's rotting fish smell."

Keith smiled. "You're a connoisseur of decaying flesh?"

"I've been around enough decaying human bodies to know the distinctive smell of rotting human flesh. We'll get a sniff of it as soon as the divers get here to recover the body."

Keith regretted his flippant comment. "Um, I'm sorry. I forgot…"

I put up my hand. "Cops do that all the time. They get stuck at a murder or the scene of a deadly accident, and the conversations wander. Sometimes it's just to pass the time. Other times it's to break the intense grief of dealing with the death of another human."

Greg nodded toward my holster. "You ever have to fire your gun?"

"We have to re-qualify quarterly."

"I mean, have you ever shot at someone?"

I flashed back to past incidents, and they played through my mind as if I were there. When I mentally returned, I realized all three were staring at me. "Sorry. It's not easy to get over taking someone's life." I glanced at Jill, who immediately looked away.

"Greg and Keith, what do you guys do when you're not babysitting people like us?"

"We're seasonal, and we spend our summers giving tours and guiding groups. In the winter, we're hooked up with a logger by Hayward, and we keep busy cutting trees and driving logging trucks."

"Sounds like a dream life," Jill said.

Keith shrugged. "It works for now. At some point, I'll have to get what my mother calls a 'grown-up' job and do the forty-hour a week thing. I suppose I'll get married and raise a couple kids."

Greg shook his head. "My folks farm in southern Wisconsin, near LaCrosse. At some point, I'll have to move back home and help my dad."

The conversation died, and Jill went to check out the fish guts. I pulled out my phone and called Margaret Steller. She answered on the second ring. "Special Agent Steller, how can I assist you?"

"I'm Doug Fletcher, from the National Park Service. Jess Pond suggested I call you about the investigation we've undertaken of the honeymooners who disappeared from the St. Croix."

I heard her keyboard clicking. "I have an email from Jess, but I hadn't opened it. It says you're from Texas and working on the St. Croix missing couple. He also says I can trust you."

I laughed. "Well, I trust Jess too. I can't say that about many of the FBI agents I've dealt with."

There was a pause, and except for the clicking keys, I thought Special Agent Steller had left. "Okay, Fletcher, I've got a follow-up email from Jess. He's got someone working on tracing a website posting for you. He is apparently handing you off to me because he asked me to tell you that whoever posted the link covered their tracks. Would you care to fill me in on what that means?"

"Actually, there's been a development in the missing honeymoon couple that will be of more interest to you. We've located a body in a backchannel of the St. Croix."

"Where are you?"

"I'm standing next to a canoe about two hundred yards from where we found a body in the water."

"How did you…?"

"It's not something I want to get into on my cellphone. We're between Osceola and Stillwater on the Wisconsin side of the St. Croix."

"I'm going to hop in my car and drive west. I'll contact Polk and St. Croix counties to see who can get someone to you quickest. I'll meet you wherever they take the body."

"Stillwater PD has the Coast Guard on the way, and my contact said she might be able to get someone from the county here quicker."

"I'll have someone ping your cellphone location, and I guarantee someone will be at your location in fifteen minutes."

"Really?"

"Sometimes the FBI can pull some strings. And by the way, when you meet me, call me Maggie. I've known Jess Pond for twenty years, and if he trusts you, that means something to me."

"I'm Doug, and my partner is Jill."

"I'm on my way."

Jill was poking in the stinking garbage can with a stick. "Look at this." She used a crook in the stick to lift the two-foot filleted carcass of a catfish out of the garbage can. Flies buzzed around her in a swarm.

Keith was reading his email and looked up. "That's a nice one."

"That explains the stink," I said.

Greg had been poking around in the weeds beside the boat launch. "Not entirely. The fisherman had been using chicken livers for bait, and he dumped them here."

Jill dropped the carcass as sirens whined in the distance. "They use chicken livers for bait?"

Greg stood up. "Yeah, the old-timers bait treble hooks with them and leave them out in the sun for a couple days. They claim they're the world's best catfish bait."

"I suppose so," I replied. "The river carries the scent, and the catfish probably come swimming like sharks responding to blood in the water."

The siren stopped about a mile away. Keith put his phone away and stood up. "The sheriff's deputy probably just turned off Highway 35. There's no need for the siren on the little dirt road that leads down here."

A brown sheriff's car eased down the rutted gravel road and parked next to Jill and the garbage can. The deputy that got out was a young woman who looked like she'd just graduated from the police academy. She was spit-polished and carried herself with authority.

"Which one of you is Fletcher?"

Jill smiled and put out her hand. "I'm Jill Fletcher." She nodded toward me. "That's Doug Fletcher."

The deputy glanced at the badge clipped to Jill's belt. "You're the National Park Service investigator who called the FBI about a dead body?"

"No, that would be Doug."

The deputy, whose name tag said Sherman, nodded and walked to me. "Dispatch had two calls—one from the Stillwater PD asking if we had a water recovery team, and one from the FBI telling us to get to this landing ASAP. What's going on?"

We gathered near the canoes. "We found a body in the channel. We couldn't recover it in the canoe, so we need support to make a recovery and get him to the medical examiner."

Deputy Sherman looked around. "Where's the body?"

"He's still in the channel. He's hooked with fishing line, and we left the bobber attached so we could direct the divers to him." I put out my hand. "Please call me, Doug."

The serious deputy put out her hand. "Dina Sherman." We made introductions all around. Then she asked, "the body isn't floating?"

"No, it's weighted down or caught on a snag. We assume it's one of the couple reported missing on Friday."

"I remember seeing a note about that."

Greg seemed quite taken with Deputy Sherman, her wavy blonde hair, and her trim figure, mostly hidden under a bulletproof vest. "I haven't seen you around. We work the Namekagon, but sometimes do tours along the St. Croix."

I could see that Deputy Sherman wasn't interested in Greg or small talk. "I just started with the sheriff's department. I'd been with the Hudson PD for the past two years." She turned her head and spoke into her radio as she walked away from us.

Jill smiled at Greg. "I don't think it's love at first sight."

Greg shrugged. "I might be able to wear down her resistance."

Deputy Sherman came back after completing her radio conversation. "Dispatch is directing the recovery team here. They'd called out the divers but weren't sure where to put their boat in. They should be here in twenty minutes or so."

"The Coast Guard is on their way up from Bayport, but they might not be here for another hour," I said. "They probably aren't equipped to make a recovery."

Sherman shook her head. "They're mostly set up for ticketing boaters without life jackets and helping disabled boats. We've got divers who've made recoveries of dead bodies."

"Is there a county coroner or medical examiner coming who can do a quick exam of the body?"

"We usually transport the bodies to him. There's not a lot of mystery in a drowning."

Jill looked at me. When I didn't immediately respond, she jumped in. "We're not sure this is a drowning. There were two people in the canoe, and we haven't had contact with either of them since Friday."

Deputy Sherman weighed Jill's comments. "I suppose the divers will have to locate the other victim. If their canoe went over back here, she's probably not too far away. The current isn't strong away from the main channel."

"There may be foul play involved. We'd like your department to check the island and shore for evidence."

The deputy looked across the channel at the brushy island. "That'll have to be the sheriff's call."

I nodded my understanding. "Please contact him or her."

Sherman studied my face for a second. "I think we should wait until the body is recovered."

"I think you should make the call now...unless you want me to contact the National Park Service superintendent or the FBI."

Sherman didn't like my suggestion. "Tell you what, Fletcher. You do your job and let me do mine."

"We've got a woman who's been missing since Friday. She may have drowned, but something else may have happened to her. She might be on that island injured, or there may be foul play involved. If you were the victim, would you like us to be standing around with our thumbs up our butts, waiting for someone to make a decision, or would you like to have every effort be made to find me?"

Sherman stiffened, then walked away, talking into her radio. I pulled out my cellphone and hit redial, hoping to get Maggie Steller somewhere between Minneapolis and Stillwater.

"Fletcher?"

"You did well. There's a Polk County deputy here, as you promised. But she's not excited about mobilizing any search efforts. She wants to wait until the body is recovered, and the divers look for the second victim. I suggested searching the shoreline and island. I also played the 'we've still got a missing woman' card, but she's unimpressed."

"Yeah, the locals don't like having a fed pushing them around. We get that all the time, and I imagine they're even less impressed with having a National Park Service ranger telling them what they should do. I'll make a call, but that may be throwing gas on the fire. In the meanwhile, try not to irritate him."

"It's a her, Deputy Dina Sherman, and I've already irritated her. She's on the radio with her dispatcher. Wait, she's switched to her cellphone."

"If she's on the phone, she may have already moved your request up the chain of command. I'll make a call to nudge them. Try not to alienate her any further."

"I'll have my female partner deal with her. Maybe they'll bond."

Maggie laughed. "Let me know how that works for you."

I walked over to Jill, who was watching Deputy Sherman. "I've pissed her off. See if you can de-escalate her irritation with the National Park Service."

"Oh, I see that going really well. You irritate her, and then you want me to act sweet and be her new buddy. Maybe I'll invite her over for coffee and cookies."

"What does Mandy do that wins people over?"

"Mandy is a southern belle who oozes charm. I'm just a South Dakota ranch girl. I doubt she'll be impressed with my horsemanship."

Deputy Sherman walked over with her cellphone in her hand. She held it out to me. "The sheriff wants to talk to you."

I took the phone. "Is he going to ream my butt?"

Sherman shrugged. "He wants to talk to you."

"This is Investigator Doug Fletcher."

"Dina says you're trying to jam us up. What the hell is going on?"

"I'm not trying to jam you up. We've got a dead body in the St. Croix. We assume it's the male of the couple who disappeared last Friday. The woman is still missing. We hope she's still alive, so I'd like to get people out here to search the shoreline and island next to the location of the body."

"You'd like to make the search belong to me."

"Sheriff, I'm with the National Park Service, and most local departments don't want us in the middle of their investigations. If you check with the Corpus Christi Police Department or the Crook County, Wyoming sheriff's department, they'll tell you about how I work with the local folks." I paused. "I'm not trying to tell you how to run this, but I'm scared to death that somebody snatched the woman. I don't want to wait around until all involved parties decide whose case it is and how we're not going to step on each other's toes. There's an FBI agent on her way, and if you've got this thing under control, she'll stand back and let you take the lead. If you're fretting and fuming about who's meddling in your county, she's going to take over and make us all look like a bunch of Keystone Kops."

"Give me a phone number for that Crook County guy, then hang loose and try not to piss off my deputy any further."

I pulled up the number on my cellphone directory and read it to him, then I ended the call and handed the phone to the deputy.

"Is your butt bleeding?" Sherman asked.

"I'm doing okay. I explained my role, and I hope we can get this off the stove."

Jill handed her cellphone to the deputy. "Take a look at this." Jill mouthed *Corpus Christi* to me.

The phone was playing the FBI news conference after the close of our case with the treasure hunters and stolen Spanish coins. Deputy Sherman's face went from disgust to resignation. She handed the phone back to Jill and looked at me. "That was you on the podium, wearing the Smokey Bear hat?"

"That was me. I…"

Jill interrupted me by handing her phone to Sherman again. This time I heard the Crook County sheriff and his deputy.

Sherman looked at Jill. "You pulled a deputy off the interstate?"

Jill nodded. "We're here to help you, not take over."

Another news conference started to play. Jill reached for her phone, but Sherman stepped back and watched. Then she looked at Jill. "I've never fired my weapon off the range. You…"

Jill put out her hand and looked embarrassed. "I did what had to be done."

Sherman looked between the two of us. "You're married."

"Yes. We're assigned to Padre Island National Seashore, but we've had a couple temporary investigative assignments, like this search for the missing couple."

Sherman's phone rang, and she handed Jill's cell back, then stepped away from us. She nodded, said yes, a lot, looked at Jill and me, then gave her phone to me. She took Jill's elbow, and they walked to the front of Sherman's car.

"This is Fletcher."

"I've got a posse, a bunch of volunteers we use to do searches and help with small-town parades. I just spoke to their lieutenant, and he's gathering them. They'll have folks there after supper and will be able to search until sunset."

"Thank you."

There was a pause. "Fletcher, I spoke with Hank, the Crook County sheriff. He says you and your wife are the real deal. If he's right, you really are here to help us and not to step all over us. I'm on my way there."

"Thank you. I'll do whatever I can to assist, but my main concern is finding the missing woman, and I won't be quiet about what I think should be done to make that happen. In the end, whatever that end might be, I'll gladly pass this off to you and fade away. I have no interest in ever being on the podium for another news conference in my life."

"My name is Jerry. May I call you Doug?"

"That's what I prefer."

"Okay, Doug. We're partners, and I'm right beside you on wanting to find the woman. My water patrol and divers are on their way. I'll be there as quick as I can. Will that work for you?"

"Thanks, Jerry." I had my finger poised to end the call when I heard my name.

"Doug, the sheriff I spoke with said you were teamed up with your wife. Is she there too?"

"Yes, Jill is talking with Deputy Sherman."

"Hank said if he ever needed someone to cover his back, he'd choose you and Jill. That's high praise from a rural sheriff."

"I'll have to thank Hank for his kindness next time I see him, and I hope I can live up to the image he has of us."

"Did Jill really shoot a running suspect who had the local deputies and FBI ducking for cover?"

"She's not proud of killing that guy. But yes, she stepped out from behind a sheltered position, fired, and hit him a dozen times as he ran from his barn to his house."

"I should have her give lessons to my deputies. They all qualify on the range, shooting at fixed silhouettes, but man, hitting a running suspect who's firing at you...that takes guts and a sharp eye. Jill must really be something."

I looked at Jill and Deputy Sherman. They were talking like old friends, smiling, and gesturing. "She is."

I handed the phone back to Deputy Sherman. "Fletcher, I'm sorry I snapped at you."

I waved off her apology. "I got in your face and was trying to dictate what you were doing. I'm sorry I came on too strong."

The deputy put out her hand. "My friends call me Dina."

I shook her hand. "I'm Doug, and you already know Jill."

"The sheriff said you two are seasoned cops, not just pushy National Park Service rangers."

"I'd like to think so."

Jill put her hand on my arm. "I'm new at this, but Doug was a St. Paul detective before he joined the National Park Service."

Dina looked impressed. "What do you think happened to the woman?"

"We don't know, but my greatest hope is that she's slightly injured, waiting for someone to find her."

"And your worst fear?"

"That the divers will find her body when they recover the man."

"There are miles of shoreline and dozens of islands between Taylors Falls and O'Brien State Park. Nearly all of it is wild and brushy. If they dumped their canoe, she could be anywhere along the way."

"Yes. That's why we were canoeing with Keith and Greg. We checked the shoreline and the backwaters down to here and didn't see anything interesting. But we're only halfway to O'Brien, and there's nothing to say she wasn't unconscious and drifting with the current in her life jacket. She might be past O'Brien."

"There are a couple of scout camps downstream."

Jill nodded. "The National Park Service contacted them and asked them to search their shoreline."

"The camp on the Wisconsin side has miles of shoreline and runs up into the bluffs. If the only person checking is the ranger, he's not going to cover all of it, especially the parts upstream. A lot of that is wild and uncut by paths, like the island. We helped them search for a couple missing scouts last year, and it was tough going."

"Did you find the missing scouts?" Jill asked.

"We did. They were holed up in an abandoned house that had been given to the scouts. They'd snuck off to smoke some marijuana. They got turned around and went north instead of south. They were mosquito-bitten, covered with ticks, and were starting to break out in poison ivy blisters. Those poor kids learned a tough lesson. I imagine their scoutmaster and parents laid into them afterward, too."

"How many old houses are there in the scout camp?" I asked.

"I don't know. There were a couple, boarded up, but you know how teenagers are, they find a way to sneak inside."

Dina's radio called her, and she walked away.

Without the need to look like the upbeat, in-control ranger, Jill slumped. "I'm dreading this. You're sure there's a body out there?"

"Oh, yeah."

"What are the odds that the woman's there too?"

"I can't give you odds on that. There are a million possibilities that put her somewhere else."

Jill glanced at Dina, who'd switched to her phone. "What are the odds that she's still alive?"

"I think you already know the answer to that."

Jill closed her eyes. "It's a recovery operation like we told Cheryl. I wish I knew where to look."

"Perk up. Here comes Dina."

"The divers just turned off the highway. They'll be here in a minute or two."

"Thanks."

"What made you pull on the fishing bobber?" Dina asked. "Was it some kind of cop intuition? I would've paddled right past it without giving it a second thought."

"It wasn't intuition, just curiosity. I got lucky...or unlucky, depending on how you view the discovery of a dead body. How long until the posse gets here?"

"They're civilians with jobs, children, and lives. We may see a few of them in an hour, but most won't be here until close to supper time."

The gravel crunched as a brown SUV towing a boat pulled into the parking area. The SUV had the sheriff's department logo. The boat was unmarked except for a hoop over the top that appeared to have red and blue flashers hidden in the framework.

We walked with Dina to the SUV, and she introduced us to two men wearing t-shirts and shorts. They wasted no time, donning black wetsuits behind the SUV and pulling out scuba gear. We stood aside as they backed the trailer to the slope leading down to the water. They parked there until they got their gear onboard, then unhooked the straps to the trailer.

Steve, the older of the two with a graying crewcut, walked to us. "Who's riding along to show us where the supposed body is?"

I glanced at Greg and quickly reasoned that he wasn't going to do well with the recovery of a "ripe" dead body. "I'm the one who found it, so I guess I'm the one who rides along. We're only going a hundred yards up this backchannel. There's a red and white fishing bobber marking the location."

"And you think there's a body there?"

"I know there's a body there."

Steve looked at my holster and badge. "Have you ever seen a dead body, Ranger Fletcher?"

"Steve, I've attended about fifty autopsies in four states. I've seen freshly dead bodies and bodies that have been nearly picked clean by coyotes and vultures. Let's go."

I got a look that said he didn't believe me. He went to his partner, and the two of them launched the boat. Steve parked the SUV and trailer. I got in the boat while Garth, who looked about twenty, held it for me.

We motored the short distance to the bobber. I glanced back at the gallery, watching from the boat launch. "Have you ever done this with an audience?"

"We've done it with news cameras running. I'm surprised some enterprising news producer hasn't caught our radio transmissions and sent out a truck," said Steve.

Garth took us near the bobber, then cut the motor. The boat moving only by the momentum carried us to the marker. Steve snatched the bobber out of the water and took up the line as the momentum carried us until the line went straight down.

Steve looked at me. "So, there's a body on the end of this line?"

"He's wearing a silver wristwatch."

Garth moved forward and dropped an anchor on the opposite side of the boat. Steve tossed the bobber back into the water, and the two men put on flippers, black neoprene gloves, and masks. Garth was picking up his air tank when Steve stopped him.

"Hang on for a minute. I'll just dive down and take a quick peek."

Steve sat on the gunwale and tipped over backward. He disappeared below the surface in a cloud of bubbles. He was back up in thirty seconds and looked at me as if considering an apology. None was offered.

"Garth, put a loop in the rope and hand it to me. Spread a tarp on the bow." He glanced at me. "This isn't going to be pretty. Put on a pair of gloves so you can help."

"Is he stuck on a branch?"

"He's got a rope tied around his ankles, and it's tied to an anchor. Someone didn't want him to float away."

"What's with the bobber?"

"It looks like someone was trying for catfish and snagged his arm with a treble hook."

Chapter Eight

I spent two hours with the sheriff's divers. After recovering the man, the divers did an underwater search in the immediate area around the recovery site. After nearly exhausting their scuba tanks, they used a sonar device to do a grid search of the entire backchannel. The sonar picked up many varieties of debris on the river bottom, most being rocks and tree trunks. They make quick dives to check on two suspicious items that turned out to be a tractor tire and a submerged log, probably dating back to the heyday of logging when the St. Croix had been used to deliver logs to downstream lumbermills.

Dozens of people showed up during our search. A few members of the sheriff's posse arrived, and half of them walked the shoreline. The other half were delivered to the island by the Coast Guard boat. They'd joined us halfway through the search and had split the search pattern with the divers, but they didn't find anything of interest on their sonar.

The body we brought to the landing wasn't pretty. Several days in the relatively warm river water made the victim grotesque and smelly. When we arrived onshore, several vehicles were in the parking lot, including a National Park

Service SUV. Cheryl stood next to a middle-aged man whose uniform had stars on his collar points. I assumed he was the sheriff.

Everyone backed away as we beached the boat. Two men in Tyvek coveralls and rubber gloves came forward with a gurney. They helped move the body out of the boat and into a body bag they loaded onto the gurney. Two sheriff's deputies helped them wheel the gurney across the gravel boat launch and parking lot to a white van.

I hung back and let the professionals deal with the body. I saw Jill and Cheryl standing together on the fringes of the crowd. Cheryl had moved forward before they'd bagged the body. I'm sure she'd hoped to identify the remains, but she turned away quickly after glancing at the dead man's face. The bloating and submersion in the water made the body unrecognizable. To her credit, she didn't get sick and asked to see the man's wedding ring and watch. Based on those and his distinctive red hair, she'd told the coroner she was ninety-nine percent certain the body was the male newlywed.

The sheriff offered his hand as I stepped out of the boat. In my younger years, I would've viewed his offer as a slight. Now, I took his hand in hopes of not doing a faceplant when I hopped to the ground. I had a sensation the ground was moving after our two hours on the rocking boat.

"Fletcher?"

"Doug, please."

The sheriff shook my hand. "Jerry Starkey."

A middle-aged woman who looked like she'd chosen her wardrobe based on the book "Dress for Success" joined us. "I'm Maggie. We spoke on the phone."

I looked around the boat landing at the jumble of police vehicles. "Where are the news vans?"

Maggie glanced at the sheriff. "We haven't notified anyone about the recovery. I imagine Jerry will have to address the press once they've got an ID of the body." When I didn't respond, she looked confused. "Is something wrong?"

"Jess Pond said you aren't a glory hound, just a hard-working law enforcement person who was happy to work behind the scenes to accomplish things."

"That was kind of him," she replied.

Jill and Cheryl joined us just as the sheriff commented. "Because we're on the Wisconsin/Minnesota border, we've dealt with Maggie a couple times. She's a team player. I hope she feels the same way about my people."

Maggie smiled. "The river isn't a hotbed of crime, but because it's an interstate waterway, there are jurisdictional issues that arise. There haven't been any disputes that I know about. We're all cops trying to solve crimes."

Cheryl stepped forward. "My brother said the FBI is monitoring his phones for a ransom demand. Has he been contacted by kidnappers?"

"I'm sorry, Cheryl. I didn't realize you had a family connection to the missing couple."

"The woman is my niece. My brother and sister-in-law adopted her from Viet Nam."

"I haven't been notified of a ransom demand or any other contact from someone who knows where your niece is."

Cheryl turned her head, and we all watched as the body was loaded into the white van. "I was scared to death that you'd found her..."

Jill put her arm around Cheryl's shoulders. "We all hope there will be a different outcome."

"Sheriff," I said, "we'll continue paddling the river from here. Do you have any suggestions about what else could be done?"

Jerry shook his head. "It would take the posse days to fight their way down the riverbanks. I could ask for community volunteers and put them on the riverbank in relays. The boat is at your disposal if you'd like to cover the riverbank faster than you can in a canoe."

I waved to Greg and Keith, our guides. "The sheriff said I could use his boat for cruising the riverbanks rather than paddling. What do you think?"

Greg looked at his partner. "I don't know how Keith feels, but I think that might be a good way to cover the main channel. I think we'd be better off using the canoes in the backwaters and around the little islands."

"Yep, the canoes can get us into places you won't want to take an outboard motor."

110

Maggie nodded toward the two Coast Guard men. "I'll talk to the Coast Guard and ask them to search below Stillwater. There are fewer backwaters down there."

I looked at the sheriff. "Jerry, what can you tell me about the scout camp on the Wisconsin side of the river?"

"Not a lot. They operate under the supervision of an on-site ranger. The boys are always with adult leaders. We've had maybe three calls from the camp since I was elected ten years ago, and two of them were rescues of kids who got injured climbing the bluffs."

"I heard there are some abandoned houses at the far north end of their property. Do you think it'd be a good idea to check them?"

Jerry smiled. "Fletcher, that is the smoothest order I've ever received. I'll see if I can free up someone to talk to the camp ranger." He looked toward Maggie, Cheryl, and me. "Some of you should talk to the people operating the old Kiwanis camp and the Catholic retreat on the Minnesota side. I don't know what they've got for outbuildings or undeveloped shoreline, but it's worth checking."

Cheryl looked stricken. "Shit, you're not going to get any help from the Coast Guard. The Secret Service will have them tied up. The President's son is coming canoeing with his class. The National Park Service will have every available resource assigned to support them."

The sheriff rolled his eyes. "Half the law enforcement people in western Wisconsin will be closing roads for his motorcade."

Maggie ran her tongue inside her lips like she had a bad taste in her mouth. "The FBI has a few people under surveillance for the next week."

Jill had never been part of the preparation for a Presidential visit and looked lost. "What are you talking about?"

"When any member of the First Family or Vice President's family travel, the Secret Service has a prep team who goes out ahead to organize security with the local agencies. They arrange to have roads closed, so the motorcades never have to slow down, they check out all the places they're going to stay and upgrade the security, they have us review the list of people who've sent threatening letters, emails, or calls and each of them gets a visit. The ones deemed to be a viable threat are detained or put under surveillance the duration of the trip."

Jill was incredulous. "That's insane."

"Yes, it is," Maggie replied. "Be glad your state isn't the home of the President or Vice President. I pity the agencies who have to deal with this every time one of the VIPs decides to come home for a holiday, birthday, or vacation."

"This is a real thing?" Jill asked.

The sheriff leaned close. "It's real. We'll have every cop and civil servant who wears a uniform on a street corner, managing the traffic control. Hell, I heard the city of Hudson has the dog catcher assigned to one intersection."

A man wearing Tyvek coveralls approached us as he pulled off his face mask and gloves. "Sheriff, if you've got a second."

Jerry waved him over to the group and introduced us. "This is Doctor Wekkin, the medical examiner who handles northwest Wisconsin." Jerry had us each give our title and agency.

The doctor looked uncomfortable, addressing all of us. "If I could have a minute of Jerry's time…"

"Stan, these folks are all stakeholders in this investigation. The National Park Service found the body. Jill and Doug Fletcher are here from Texas to investigate the disappearance of the couple."

"Sorry to swamp you with people," I said. "Can you give us a preliminary cause of death and your impressions?"

"I'd prefer to reserve my thoughts until after the post-mortem exam."

The sheriff cut off my response, which was going to be impolite and direct. "I know you don't like to speculate, but that guy's wife is still missing, and we'll have thirty or forty people combing the river and shoreline tomorrow. Is there anything you can give us that will help us focus our efforts?"

"Who was with the recovery team?"

"I was with the sheriff's divers," I said. "I saw the rope tied around his ankles and the anchor."

The medical examiner nodded. "Did you notice the contusion on the back of his head?"

"No."

The doctor shook his head. "This is why I hate speculating. There are several mitigating factors. It appears his head injury was perimortem. I won't know if it was the cause of death until I open his skull. I sense that it wasn't severe enough to be fatal, but it may have incapacitated him. He may have drowned then if he fell into the water. Or, it may have rendered him unconscious, and then parties unknown tied the anchor around his ankles and dropped him in the river where he drowned. Or, he may have died from some other cause, making the rope and anchor just a means of disposal. Whatever the cause of his death, his killer or killers didn't want the body found. I think there's something more in play than we know about."

"What do you mean?" Jill asked.

"If this was a robbery, why not disable him, take his valuables, and leave him on a secluded island. It might easily be hours or a day before he'd be located and rescued. By then, they'd be long gone. If they'd drowned him or let him drown, his body would've been suspended in the water until gases built up and floated him to the surface. That would've given them several days to escape or even fence things they'd stolen before they'd be reported missing. The killer didn't want his body found. Why?"

Dr. Wekkin walked away, apparently having shared as much as he felt necessary.

I looked at Cheryl. "Is there something special about your niece?"

"She was cute, smart, and motivated."

"What did she do for a living?"

"She'd worked her way up through the ranks at one of the big-box retailers. Her title was assistant buyer. As far as I know, that meant she worked sixty hours a week with no overtime pay and a few benefits. She wasn't rich or famous."

"How about her parents or your brother and sister-in-law, are they wealthy?"

Cheryl cringed, obviously uncomfortable with that topic. "He does something for a company that builds thermostats and electronics. We don't talk money much, but I know he's been putting money into his 401k account. His wife works for the post office. They're not rich. We inherited a little money when our parents died, but we're not talking millions of dollars. Besides, no one has called with a ransom demand."

We moved, so the sheriff's divers could back their trailer into the river. Maggie and Cheryl went over to the two young Coast Guard men talking to Greg and Keith, apparently to update them on the plan for tomorrow.

The sheriff watched the divers load the boat on the trailer. "What do you two think?"

I nodded at Jill, allowing her to speak before I steered the conversation. It was something I'd learned in the National Guard—having the most junior people speak first allowed them to express an opinion without knowing if it aligned with their superiors. It sometimes yielded unexpected results and often brought viewpoints that would otherwise not make it to the table.

"The medical examiner's comments were interesting. I don't know what to make of them, but it made me consider why someone wouldn't want the guy's body found in terms of what it means regarding the woman. As Cheryl said, no one's called in a ransom demand, so whatever is going on has nothing to do with getting money from her parents." Jill paused and drew a deep breath, then blew it out. "I hate to consider it, but there's the possibility they killed the husband and raped her. Is her body on one of these little islands? Did they take her somewhere else?"

The sheriff listened and continued to watch the divers strap down the boat and stow their gear. "I hate to think about that possibility, but you're probably right, Jill, that may be what happened. I'd been trying to think about some other reason they'd take her away and where they might've gone. It'd be risky to bring her to a big boat launch or marina unless they had a big cabin cruiser where they could take her below and control her. But the questions are where and why."

They looked at me like they expected the correct answer. "I don't know. I have a hard time believing this is something other than a crime of opportunity. Setting up the logistics of intercepting them on the water, killing the husband, and taking off with the woman would take a lot more planning than most criminals are capable of."

Cheryl and Maggie joined us at the end of my opinion. "I missed what had been said before Doug," Maggie said. "I agree with Doug's comments about most criminals not being smart. That said, there's the elephant in the room. The President's kid is coming. Is someone planning to leverage her disappearance to get to him?"

"How would they do that?" Jill asked.

"I have no idea, but we've got to keep that in mind. For now, I think we should go ahead with the plans we set for tomorrow, then reassess tomorrow night."

The sheriff looked at Maggie. "You haven't said much about the FBI's role in this."

"I've got my people with Cheryl's brother and also monitoring the internet for mention of her name or posting of her picture. I think that's a better use of their time than walking the shoreline."

I nodded. "As much as I'd like to see an army of FBI agents out here getting poison ivy while they trudge through the underbrush, I have to agree that it's more useful having them deployed in a totally different direction than the rest of us."

Cheryl looked at her watch. "I told Keith and Greg to load the canoes on my SUV. I'll drive back to the visitor center and call it a day. Doug and Jill, if you want to continue, Keith and Greg will be ready tomorrow morning. If you've got other things to pursue, I'll grab two other rangers and put them on the river with Keith and Greg. What do you think, Jerry?"

"Tomorrow's Thursday, so I might be able to get a bunch of volunteers out to walk the shoreline." He looked at me. "I think Doug and Jill should go to the scout camps, the marinas, the Catholic retreat, and the farmhouses along the river. We've got the river covered, and maybe you two can stir up something by looking in a different direction." He smiled, then added, "And I have no jurisdiction on the other side of the river, so if you could get Washington County and the Stillwater PD involved, that'd be great."

Chapter Nine

Jill drove, and I started making calls. Sandy Prudhomme's phone rolled over, and I left her a message. I'd hoped to leverage her contacts with the Washington County sheriff's department, so I was at a dead end, short of dialing 911 to contact the dispatcher.

I punched in Jess Pond's number at the Rapid City FBI office. Still at work, he picked up immediately, being one hour earlier in the mountain time zone.

"Making any headway, Doug?"

"We recovered the body of the male honeymooner. Still no sign of the woman."

"That's headway. Did his body give you any direction in finding her?"

I spent ten minutes updating him on the search, the recovery, and the plan going forward. "Did your people make any headway with the porn site?"

"We contacted the webmaster and asked for the identity of the person who put up the post. He's somewhere in Eastern Europe and wasn't particularly impressed by a call from the U.S. FBI. We're working through some folks in Interpol, but it's not going to be a priority for them, and I can't really blame them. The

Brazilian government just gave them a list of Nazis who'd escaped to South America, and their computer people are leaning on Swiss banks to find any accounts associated with names in hopes of repatriating money to the families of Jewish holocaust victims. I have a hard time arguing for prioritization of finding who posted compromising pictures over the Nazi issue."

"That's a dead end."

Jess paused. "I didn't say that. I said Interpol was a dead end. My guy found some information associated with the post. I'm not even going to pretend I understand what he said, but the bottom line is there may be a way to find out where the post originated."

"Thanks. Maggie Steller came through for us today. She seems like a solid person who's got a history of being a team player. Her people are working the computers on this end, and she helped us leverage some local resources. Thanks for connecting us."

"See, sometimes the FBI can be helpful."

"And sometimes they can be a pain in the ass."

We laughed, and I ended the call.

Jill looked at the clock on the dashboard. "It's almost seven, and I'm starving. Are you planning to feed me, or should I stop at a gas station and buy granola bars?"

"I made reservations for the fondue dinner at the Inn."

"I can't remember the last time I ate fondue. Wait, yes, it was when I was in college. What time are the reservations?"

"Fifteen minutes ago."

Jill glanced at me. "How far are we from Stillwater?"

"Probably fifteen minutes."

I pulled up the Inn's number and was assured they'd be able to accommodate us whenever we arrived. Jill listened to my end of the conversation. "I hope you've factored in a shower and change of clothes."

I sniffed my shirt. "Am I a little gamy?"

"Gamy doesn't start to describe your stink. You may have to burn your clothes. You smell like a combination of dead fish and a dead body."

"I've got news for you, honey. You were digging in the barrel with the dead catfish, and you don't smell like a rose garden either."

"How can you tell over your own stink?"

We parked in the ramp and bypassed the lobby on our way to our room. Jill was in the shower before I could strip off my clothes and stuff them into a plastic laundry bag. She popped out with her head wrapped in a towel. "I left a little hot water for you."

When I came out of the shower, Jill was already in a sundress, apparently including underwear her friend Mandy had chosen as an alternative to Jill's usual sports bra and grannie panties. The neckline of her dress exposed a tantalizing hint of cleavage.

"I take it you approve of my outfit?"

"I'm willing to skip supper."

Jill walked to the door and put her hand on the knob. "Uh, uh. I'm starving."

* * *

The Matterhorn Room was subdued with people at a dozen tables, sipping wine and dipping shrimp and meat into fondue pots of hot oil. The maître d seated us, and a young man appeared with bottles of wine.

"Red or white?"

Jill smiled. "Can we see a menu first?"

"The menu is set. Your only choice is between shrimp or beef."

"I guess I'll have a glass of white wine and the shrimp."

The waiter poured for Jill. "And you, sir?"

"I'll have a glass of sparkling water and the beef."

"Certainly, but the wine is included as part of your dinner."

Jill was enjoying herself, watching me wrestle between not drinking much and being too cheap to not drink wine that was part of the price of my dinner.

"Red, please."

We touched our wine glasses. "Did you see the dinner price?" she asked.

"I'm sure our per diem won't cover this."

She sipped her wine. "I don't care. After today, I deserve whatever this is costing you."

"Costing me?"

Jill batted her eyes. "Don't you think I'm worth it?"

I reached out and squeezed her hand. "You already know that answer."

Our waiter smiled when he delivered two plates with snail shells, tiny forks, and little grippers to hold the shells. He set the plates in front of us. The expression on Jill's face was priceless but not lost on our waiter.

"Would you like me to demonstrate how to remove the escargot from the shell?"

Jill answered without looking up. "Sure."

After the waiter left, Jill sat with the tiny fork in her hand, a snail speared on the tines. She leaned close. "Snails. Really?"

I put the morsel in my mouth, enjoying the buttery garlic flavor. "It's good."

Jill looked skeptical.

"You're not in South Dakota anymore."

Jill put the escargot in her mouth and chewed tentatively. A smile spread over her face, and her dimples appeared. "I've got to tell Mom about this."

We ate supper, talking about anything other than the investigation. Jill's phone rang as our fondue pot arrived. I'd left my phone on the charger in the room and tried to stop her from answering hers, fearing it was someone about to drag us away from our romantic dinner.

Jill checked the caller ID and answered, "Hi, Ronnie."

I got half of the brief conversation, which ended with the comment, "We're planning on it."

Jill ended the call and turned off the phone. "Ronnie reminded me about the family reunion."

"No."

"I already said yes."

"You can go if you want to. I'll stay here."

A platter of cubed steak and shrimp arrived. We were served another glass of wine and waited for the waiter to leave.

Jill put her hand on mine. "We'll talk about it later."

"There's nothing to discuss. I'm not going."

Jill's dimples appeared. "You'll change your mind."

"I doubt it."

She leaned close and whispered, "I've got a nightgown in the room that'll change your mind."

I chuckled. "You're not playing fair. You know what buttons to push."

"There are no buttons. There is *a* button. It's the same one you used on me when you convinced me to spend a week with you in San Antonio."

The waiter cleared our dishes and poured Jill another glass of wine. I switched to tonic and lime, and our conversation switched to our families, each with their own foibles. The waiter delivered dessert—grapes coated with sour cream and sprinkled with brown sugar. The horrors of the day faded away as Jill kidded me and laughed. Her dimples somehow took me to a happy, safe place where only the two of us existed. A place I'd lost when I'd been a St. Paul cop, and a place Jill hadn't been in since her childhood.

We walked through the lobby holding hands.

The desk clerk waved at me. "Mr. Fletcher, there's a message for you. A gentleman called and said that you're not answering your cellphone."

I put the message in my pocket and took Jill's hand.

"Aren't you going to read it?" Jill asked as we waited for the elevator.

"Not until morning."

"It might be important."

The elevator door opened, and a couple walked out before we entered. "Nothing's going on that's more important than…"

Jill pulled me close. "Nothing more important than us?"

I didn't answer as we walked to our room. Inside, I locked the door and pocketed the key. "My priorities were mixed up for a while. You've helped me get them straight again. You're first, and everything else comes after that."

Jill pulled me close. "*We're* first. Jobs, family, the rest of the world, all come somewhere else down the list."

"You were going to show me a nightgown."

Jill slipped out of my arms and opened her suitcase. She held something hidden in her hand and turned to me. "Are you going to stay awake long enough for me to scrub my face and slip into this?"

"I'll try."

I was watching The Late Show in our darkened room when Jill slipped out of the bathroom. Her trim figure was silhouetted by the bathroom light for a second before it went dark. She took the remote from me and switched off the television, then snuggled against me under the covers.

"Do you like my nightgown?"

"Is it something you and Mandy picked out?"

"We found it in a Corpus Christi mall. Mandy said it's the kind of thing nice girls don't admit to owning."

"It's much more seductive than the long flannel nightgown you wore in South Dakota."

Jill kissed my neck. "That was meant to keep me warm. Mandy said this is meant to be ripped off my body in a fit of passion."

"Let's not rip it off. I think it should be worn over and over…"

* * *

The glowing red numerals on the alarm clock said 6 a.m. when the phone rang. I didn't remember leaving a wake-up call and would certainly not have asked the front desk to call me at six.

"Fletcher."

"Doug, where the hell are you?"

I rubbed the sleep from my eyes. "I'm in bed asleep. Who is this?"

"It's Maggie. Why didn't you call when you got my message last night?"

"I didn't get your message last night."

"Turn on your damned cellphone. Your inbox is probably overflowing."

I disconnected the charger and powered it up. "What's going on?" I asked as it went through the start-up mode. Jill got out of bed and dashed to the bathroom.

"The shit hit the fan after the sheriff announced the recovery of the man's body from the river. The Secret Service is bouncing off the walls and wants the woman found. Yesterday would be better than today."

My phone finally went to log in, and I entered my password. As soon as the password was accepted, it started pinging like rapid sonar. "Looks like I have a few voicemail messages."

"Let me spare you answering the dozen or so I left since eight last night. The Secret Service called the FBI, telling us to get engaged in this case. Of course, the FBI person they spoke with in Washington was at a level so high that he didn't even know what case they were talking about. The calls trickled down to my special agent in charge, who asked me for an update. When he found out the body was recovered in the St. Croix River, he called the Coast Guard because it's an interstate waterway. Then he asked if it was in the part of the river managed by the park service. I said it was, so he called the park service in Washington. You know how feds love to spread the joy around, and having you involved gives him someone else to tee off on. Geez, it's become an alphabet soup of federal agencies, and we're going to step on each other."

I waited for Maggie to slow down enough so I could ask a question. Jill emerged from the bathroom with wet hair and wore her green and gray National Park Service uniform.

"Slow down, Maggie. Jill's here with me, so I'm putting you on speaker. Have there been any developments in the case overnight?"

"Nothing, except people with their undies in a bunch, calling all over the FBI, National Park Service, Coast Guard, sheriff's departments, and the medical examiner, placing pressure on each other to find the woman or figure out what happened to her before the President's kid shows up for a canoe trip."

"Okay, before I listen to my voicemails, is there any change in what Jill and I are doing?"

Maggie blew out a breath. "No. Go ahead and check with the scouts and the Catholic retreat as planned but get your butts in gear."

"What's happening with the other agencies?"

"You'll have a message from the Polk County sheriff. He's mobilized people in every adjacent county and the regional SWAT team. There will be people tripping over each other, searching the riverbanks. Cheryl's pulling park service people from everywhere she can reach to search the islands. The Minnesota State Patrol has their plane up, checking from the air, and tonight the National Guard will have a helicopter up with forward-looking infrared to search through the tree canopy and fields around the river. They think the FLIR might light up if there's a body decomposing and not buried too deep. The Coast Guard will have boats searching the water and shore from the Iowa border to Stillwater." She paused. "Did I leave anyone out?"

Jill stepped closer to the phone. "How about the FBI?"

"We've got computer searches running with keywords and a description of the woman. If there are any cellphone calls, social media posts, or dating websites commenting on her or anyone matching her description, we'll have people knocking on doors."

"Sounds like an army is being mobilized."

"Oh, the Army reserve offered to bring in people from Fort McCoy, Wisconsin. Any ground we haven't covered with other resources by Saturday, the Army will search."

"I'm going to shower, and then I'll check my messages."

"Run a comb through your hair and have Jill drive while you listen to the messages."

"Anything else?" I asked, too sharply.

"Do. Not. Turn. Off. Your. Phone."

I hung up without answering.

Jill saw me burning. "Easy. She's only reacting to the pressure she's getting. It's not like she's ordering us to do anything we didn't have planned, and she's laid all her cards on the table."

I was ready to go on a tirade, but the room phone rang while my hand was still on it. "Fletcher."

"Doug, I've been trying to reach you."

I pressed the speaker option. "My cellphone was off. Now it's on. What can I do for you, Cheryl?"

"I've been downstairs for two hours. Your cellphone is off. The desk clerk wouldn't call your room before six, and he wouldn't give me your room number."

"We're just getting dressed. We'll be down in a few minutes. Meet us in the dining room."

"Um…this would be better if we spoke in private."

Jill spun the phone toward her. "I'm dressed. Doug's going to jump in the shower. Come on up." Jill gave her our second-floor room number and hung up.

I pulled clothes out of my suitcase and went into the bathroom. "This is out of control," I said as I closed the door.

I heard voices when I turned off the shower. I was pulling on pants when I heard a knock on the door and the squeak of a room service cart. Jill and Cheryl were drinking coffee and eating

Danish when I opened the bathroom door. Cheryl looked tired and rumpled. I wondered if she was still in the uniform she'd worn yesterday.

Jill poured coffee for me and held out a mug. "There's been a change of plans."

I sat on the edge of the bed. "We're not going to the scout camps?"

Cheryl looked up from her coffee. "My brother called last night. He had a ransom demand and was told not to contact the police."

"Cheryl, the FBI listened to the call. It's their case."

She looked at me with tired eyes. "I trust you and Jill and your discretion."

"How much are they asking, and does your brother have access to enough money?"

"They don't want money."

I glanced at Jill, who'd apparently heard the story. She discreetly waved her hand, signaling for my patience.

"What do they want?"

"They want him to deliver the avionics software for the next generation of Air Force jets."

I opened my mouth but couldn't come up with a thing to say except, "Shit."

"They delivered a cellphone to him at work, and it rang almost as soon as he opened the courier's package. They told him what they wanted, and they let Janet say a few words."

"How and when is he supposed to make the delivery?"

"He's supposed to email a zip file to them. They'll release Janet when they receive it and authenticate the content."

I closed my eyes and considered all the things that could go wrong. "There's no way to assure they'll release your niece once they get the information."

"They told him they'd hand her a cellphone in a very public place and let her talk to him as they reviewed the authenticity of the file."

"It used to be so much easier before the internet age. People would demand money, there'd be a drop somewhere, and the victim would be turned over." I thought but didn't say that half the time, the kidnapped victim was dead before the drop.

Jill waited for Cheryl to say more, but there was no more forthcoming. "There are going to be hundreds of people wasting time searching for Janet, and we know they're not going to find her. Is there some way we can stop the search?"

Cheryl's eyes were pleading. "We can't stop the search. If we do, they'll know the FBI has been contacted, and they'll kill Janet."

"I agree. It'll be a waste of a lot of resources, but the search is very public and visible. It has to go ahead as planned. I think we have to let the FBI handle this. They'll continue to monitor the cellphone calls and the electronic pathway of the information. We can't do that."

Cheryl put up her hand. "Absolutely not! If I'd thought you were going to leave this to the FBI, I wouldn't have come to you."

"Okay. Let me think and talk at the same time. First, I'm just a cop who's spent my career chasing down low-life criminals. They tend to be pretty one dimensional and are either trying to get cash to support their drug habits, want money so they don't have to do real work, or are part of a gang.

"Secondly, I'm not a chess player and don't need to think more than a move or two ahead to anticipate what the criminals are going to do. Whatever is going on with your brother is more complicated than I…we can handle. Whoever is running this has international connections and probably has electronic savvy and monitoring capabilities. That's way out of my wheelhouse.

"Thirdly, this may not be what it seems to be. Getting back to my chess analogy, what if this is a diversion? Maybe the kidnappers are after something different. Suppose this is a gambit, and they're leaking this information to the FBI so it'll draw them away from something else, like the arrival and security of the President's son. They may be so far ahead of my thinking that we'll be chasing the laser dot like a cat while they're robbing the house."

Cheryl set her cup down on the cart and stood up. "Forget it. I'm sorry I wasted your time."

Jill stood, blocking Cheryl's path to the door. "Sit down. We're involved, and Doug's just talking through the things bouncing around inside his head."

Cheryl looked at me. "Are you in this?"

"You've opened Pandora's box, and we can't un-hear what you told us. We just need to sort out the best way of proceeding." Cheryl didn't sit and seemed ready to bolt for the door. "Cheryl, we're in your corner. Remember that we're also part of the National Park Service, and our jobs are focused on supporting you." I gestured toward the chair, and she sat down.

Jill topped off Cheryl's coffee and handed her the mug. "We're brainstorming. Work with us."

Cheryl looked unconvinced but sat. "So, what are you...we going to do?"

"As I told you, I'm talking and thinking at the same time, and I don't have a plan. Is there anything else your brother told you?"

Cheryl looked like she was replaying the conversation in her head. "We didn't talk that long..."

Jill had the quintessential question: "Why did he call you?"

"I...I think he just needed to talk to someone."

"Does he have access to the programs the kidnappers want?"

"He's the vice president of research. He's not directly involved in the programming, but I assume he has access to all their information."

"Are you two close?" Jill asked. "Does he call you often to talk about work?"

Cheryl shook her head. "Our parents died a few years ago, and we get together for Christmas, but we don't talk often. The only reason I know he's a vice president is because my sister-in-law was bragging about the stock options he gets."

I took a Danish from the tray and thought. "Is there someone at work who would benefit from him being fired?"

"I have no idea what his work environment is or who would be in line to succeed him if he left or was fired."

Jill looked startled. "Maybe it's not an international conspiracy. I wonder if a competitor would benefit from the programs he's being asked to divulge?"

Cheryl was obviously overwhelmed. "How would we sort that out?"

I finished my Danish and wiped my fingers on a napkin. "What number did your brother call from?"

"I don't think he wants me to give it to anyone."

I raised my eyebrows. "That may be what he intended exactly when he called you."

Jill leaned back. "Okay, so we're playing chess here. Maybe he bought the disposable phone assuming the kidnappers would be able to listen in. He called you because they'd know you were a relative, not a cop, and the conversation would seem innocuous. Maybe he intended to trigger you to get someone involved."

"Do you think they followed me here?"

"Only an organization as big as the FBI would have the resources to reach out that far.

Let's assume they're monitoring him so he can't make a call without it being overheard, but he really wants to get the FBI involved."

Jill pulled her cellphone out of her pocket and punched in a number. "I'm sure they're not monitoring my phone or the Rapid City FBI office." Jill put her phone on speaker and set it on the room service cart.

"Jill Fletcher? Do you have any idea what time it is here? I'm in the mountain time zone, and it's an hour earlier than you whether you're in Minnesota or Texas."

Jill smiled. "Good morning, Jess. I have a hypothetical question for you regarding a hypothetical kidnapping."

"Couldn't your hypothetical question wait until I'd had some coffee?"

"Jess, this is Doug. It's me who has the question."

"Hang on while I move to the kitchen so my wife can go back to sleep until some reasonable hour of the morning." We waited, hearing doors close and water running. "Okay. I've got coffee started. What's your hypothetical question?"

"Suppose we learned that the missing person case we are working on was, in fact, a kidnapping and that the kidnappers were asking the victim's father to give them secret avionics programs. The information may have been leaked to the victim's aunt, who was warned not to involve the police, but there's a chance his phone call was being monitored, and he was

136

attempting to alert her to get the police or FBI involved."

"And the aunt came to you with this hypothetical scenario and not the FBI?"

"Let's say the aunt works for the National Park Service, didn't know where to turn, but trusts Jill and me."

I heard a hiss as Jess' coffee pot ended its brew cycle. A cupboard creaked and closed. "Hypothetically, my South Dakota FBI contact would hear that information and say to himself, gee whiz, if I were told about a kidnapping in a different jurisdiction and didn't pass that information to the local FBI office, I'll be fired. Hypothetically speaking."

Cheryl looked like she was going to cry. Jill leaned close to the phone. "Can we have an off-the-record discussion?"

"Hell no! Jill, I'm an FBI agent, and ignoring this phone call, even though I'm in Rapid City, would end my career, probably cost me my pension, and might land me in Leavenworth. We cannot have this discussion and pretend I didn't hear anything."

Jill looked at me with pleading eyes, and I shook my head. "Jess, this is Doug."

"I was wondering if that was your heavy breathing in the background."

"How do we deal with this?"

"Hang up the phone and call Maggie Steller. Tell her about your hypothetical situation and let her bring in the resources you need to investigate this."

"Do you have a backchannel way to contact her? The call to the aunt was made from a disposable phone, and we suspect the call may have been monitored. I'm paranoid about this and what communications may be compromised."

"Are you getting paranoid?"

"Yes."

"Call her from a landline. Calls in and out of the FBI switchboard are scrambled."

"All I've got is her cellphone number."

"That's secure, too, although your cellphones can be monitored. Call her from your hotel and tell her what's up. She'll be discreet once she gets through reaming your butt for not calling her first."

"I did call her first. This call never happened."

Jess laughed. "Like hell, it didn't happen. I'll have to file a report of contact and include the details of our discussion."

"Can you delay that until we talk to Maggie?" Jill asked.

"Well, I'm at home. I can only fill out the report on my secure work computer. Once I get to the office, I meet with my agents to review the overnight activities. Then I'll have to get coffee. It'll be a while."

"Can't you have a leisurely breakfast and do the crossword puzzle before you check-in at the office?"

"Don't push it, Jill. If you call Maggie now, you'll be covered."

I picked up the phone and shut off the speaker function. "Thanks, Jess."

"Listen, Doug, you know what has to happen. Why'd you drag me into your mess?"

"Jill called in the hope her friendship might trump the FBI bureaucracy."

"I appreciate that, but I'm part of the bureau, and all your friendship is going to buy is an hour to contact Maggie."

I disconnected the call and pulled up Maggie's number on my cellphone, then used the Inn's phone to dial her number.

"Special Agent Steller. How can I help you?"

"Hi Maggie, you didn't recognize the Inn's phone number on your caller ID?"

There was a pause. "No, I didn't. What's up?"

"Cheryl is in our room. She got a call about a ransom demand last night."

"What? Cheryl got a ransom demand?"

"I'm putting you on speaker. No, she got a call from her brother, who received a ransom demand and orders not to involve the police."

"How…we've been monitoring her brother's phones."

I explained the tortuous path the information traveled to get to us, then begged her not to get the local police involved.

Maggie laughed. "As I recall, it was Doug Fletcher who complained about being cut out of FBI information."

Jill smiled. "I think he gets that now. Can you help with this?"

"Of course, I can, Jill. That's my job. Hang on while I make some notes."

"Cheryl's next to me. She might be able to explain it more completely than Doug and I can."

Cheryl repeated the story with Maggie asking questions for clarification.

"Okay, guys, this is a big pile of stinking manure. As Cheryl explained, the kidnappers don't want police involvement. I won't intervene in the search operations. I'm going to my information technology people with this, and they'll start checking international cellphone and email conversations. I'm going to pull off the people who've been monitoring your brother's phones and give them the cellphone number you gave me. I'm driving to your brother's office. I'll get there unannounced, but I don't want to risk a call." Maggie paused. "Are you still there, Cheryl?"

"Yes."

"Call your brother's disposable phone. Tell him that you and your daughter Maggie are coming over for 'take your daughter to work day,' and that you'll be there in half an hour."

"I don't have a daughter."

"It doesn't matter. I assume he's smart, and that information will tip him off to expect a visit from someone named Maggie. I can meet him in a secure meeting room and get all the details

140

without an electronic trail. Is there anything else?"

I turned off the speaker. "I assume you can do this without tipping off the kidnappers?"

"It's what we do, Doug."

"What should we do?"

"Do what we'd planned, so the kidnappers don't see us changing direction. The one thing I'd add when you're asking questions is if someone saw a woman being taken forcibly off the river."

"Got it. Will you tell us what's going on?"

"Do you promise not to call the media?"

"There's no need for me to make that call if we're part of the team."

"Fair enough."

"Maggie, one other thing. When you have the news conference, I want Cheryl on the steps with you, and I want the National Park Service mentioned as one of the lead agencies in solving the kidnapping."

"Sure. Let's hope we're there to announce the happy release of the victim and not the recovery of her body."

"Amen."

I hung up, and Cheryl was frowning. "What did you say 'amen' to?"

"The happy ending of this investigation."

Cheryl nodded. Jill looked skeptical like she expected me to explain further after Cheryl leaves.

"Maggie says we should all go on with our plans in case the kidnappers are watching. Jill and I will go downstairs and have breakfast. You go back to the park and get the rangers on the river. Tell them to watch for places other than boat launches, where the kidnappers might've pulled their boat out of the water or where they might've taken your niece ashore and loaded her into a vehicle."

Cheryl got up and brushed crumbs off her green uniform pants. "I feel guilty having all those people searching for Janet, knowing that she's been taken somewhere else."

I opened the door for Cheryl. "We don't know where she's being held. For all we know, she could be in a house along the bluffs."

Jill's eyes went wide. "I wonder if there's a way to know if someone's rented a house along the bluff or an Airbnb recently."

Cheryl brightened. "I have a girlfriend who's a real estate agent. I can ask her to do a discreet check."

Cheryl left, and I closed the door. Jill sat on the bed. "What are the odds that Janet is being held close to the river?"

"Probably one in a million, but it gives Cheryl a mission, and if the kidnappers are watching, they'd see that as a logical thing for the cops to do while they're looking for a missing woman."

Chapter Ten

While I listened to messages on my cellphone from angry and frustrated people, Jill drove us to the scout camp on the east side of the river. They'd started about the time we were eating dessert and continued until midnight. By then, I assumed that the callers had gotten the idea I couldn't answer the phone or return messages. They started again at five o'clock and continued right up to the time that Maggie convinced the front desk to put a call through to our room, probably by using the threat of her FBI position.

The one surprising call was from my mother. "Call me when you get a moment. I spoke with Jill, and she's excited about the family reunion. I'll give you details later." It was more succinct than her usual messages and using Jill as leverage was new. It was also hard to ignore because I had the cellphone on speaker, so I had my hands free to make notes.

"It sounds like Ronnie is excited about having us attend the reunion."

"I don't want to go. Maybe you can meet her somewhere, and the two of you can attend together. I'll do something else." I couldn't come up anywhere that wasn't a bar. It made me

143

aware of how far my life had sunk before moving to Arizona after my divorce.

"You'll what?"

"They always have the reunion at the zoo. You can meet relatives with Mom. I'll go watch the apes and feed the seals."

The next message was from Matt Mattson, our boss. "I guess you really are celebrating the honeymoon you missed. Glad you had the foresight to turn off your phone for the night. Call me."

The next call was also from Matt. "I don't know what you stepped in, but it must be bad based on the number of calls I'm getting."

The following one was also from Matt. "Okay, if you don't return the calls you're getting from Cheryl Britton and the FBI, there will be someone knocking on your motel door."

The last two were memorable. The first was from Maggie Steller. "Damn you, Fletcher. I was going to send an FBI ERT team to break down your motel room door, but no one seems to know where you're staying. Return my call."

"Doug, this is Matt, again. I haven't told anyone where you're staying, but if the FBI doesn't find you soon, they're threatening to check your credit card activity and send someone there. I need to talk to you."

Jill glanced at me as we crossed the new Stillwater bridge. "Call Matt. He needs to know what's going on."

I dialed his home number, reasoning that it was barely eight o'clock and he'd probably be

144

on his way to the park and wouldn't answer his cellphone while he was driving. His wife, Mandy, answered. As always, her southern accent was as sweet as honey.

"Well, the lost have been found. How are y'all? Honeymoon going well?"

I knew Matt had shared everything he was hearing. Mandy was too smooth to have her sarcasm come through over the phone, but I knew she was needling me about not returning the calls.

"The honeymoon is wonderful. We haven't left the room in two days, and the nightie you and Jill picked out, well, let's say it wasn't on her very long."

I got a jolt in my ribs from Jill's elbow. "Don't believe a thing he says," she yelled so Mandy could hear her.

"I do believe you may be stretching the truth, Ranger Fletcher."

"Is Matt still at home?"

"He left an hour ago to make calls from the office in an attempt to cover your flagging behind." Mandy paused. "Before you end the call and dial him, hand the phone to your lovely bride."

"Based on the intensity of the messages, I think it'd be best if…"

"Douglas, remember that you're speaking with Matt's boss. It'd be best if you did as I've asked." Her words were sweet and came in her lilting Texas twang, but the threat was less than candid. If I didn't give the phone to Jill, Mandy could make my life hell.

I handed the phone to Jill. "Hi, Mandy."

I couldn't hear Mandy's voice over the road noise, but I assumed the topic of the nightie came up because Jill blushed and said, "Yes, it was."

Their conversation went on until we had passed through Houlton, Wisconsin. Jill glanced at me. "Ronnie invited us to a family reunion, and Doug is being a jerk about it."

Jill handed the phone to me. "Hi, Mandy."

"Douglas, don't make me come up there and set you straight about who makes decisions about attending family functions."

"It's *my* family. I should decide if I want to go or not."

"Listen carefully. Ronnie wants to show Jill off to your family. Let her. Is that clear?"

"Yes, ma'am."

"Okay. Now hand the phone back to Jill."

I held the phone out to Jill, who took it, listened for a second, then jabbed me in the ribs. She smiled and handed the phone back to me.

"What was that all about?" I asked.

"If you give me a snarky, 'Yes, ma'am' again, I'll break one of your ribs. Got it, Fletcher?"

"I suppose 'yes, dear' would be as bad."

"What do you think, Douglas?" She paused. "Now hang up and call Matt. He's dying to know what's going on."

The sign for the scout camp turnoff came into view before I could call Matt. "Turn left. You'll get to a parking lot in about a quarter mile. Skip the parking lot on the hilltop and go right, down the steep driveway to the house at the bottom."

I punched in Matt's office number. It rang six times, and I was about to end the call when he picked up.

"Mattson."

"You sound like you just came back from a run."

I heard Matt's door close. "I was in the gift shop when I heard the phone. What are you up to? I had half a dozen calls overnight, asking how to contact you after calls to your cell rolled over to voicemail."

"Yesterday was a hell of a day. Jill and I went out for supper. My phone was dead, so I plugged it into the charger and left it in the room." I told Matt about the discovery and recovery of the male honeymooner, the FBI mobilizing the searches along the river, and Jill and me being dispatched to interview the camp leaders.

We got to the parking lot, and a hundred scouts were unloading gear from vehicles and lining up to walk down the hill to the campground.

I held the phone aside. "Go straight across and take the driveway down the hill."

"Sorry. We're at the scout camp, and Jill's doing a slalom around the groups."

"I got a call from Maggie Steller with the Minneapolis FBI. She said the President's son is coming to the park for a canoe trip, and the Secret Service has a bee in their bonnet over the missing woman. They're apparently afraid her disappearance is somehow linked to the son's trip, and they've ordered her to solve the case."

Jill turned onto the one-lane driveway and was stuck behind a group of scouts with backpacks, walking down the hill. We idled along at their walking speed, descending the long slope from the bluffs to the flat land along the river where the camp had dozens of cabins, two lodges, and a few campgrounds.

"Cheryl Britton was in the lobby this morning and came up to our room as soon as the desk clerk would let her call. The missing woman is her niece, and it's complicated, but her brother received a ransom demand." I explained the scenario to Matt as Jill fumed about the scouts not letting her pass.

We found another smaller parking lot at the bottom of the hill. "Matt, we're at the campground, so I'm going to end the call."

"Keep me posted." He paused. "I assume the FBI and National Park Service know where you're staying now, so they can send someone to knock on the door if your phone is off."

"I'm afraid so."

Jill parked next to a railing, and we got out of the car. Scouts milled around sorting out which trail they were taking to their cabins and campsites.

I pointed to a house behind a split-rail fence, painted to blend in with the trees and limestone bluffs. "That's the ranger's house. I don't imagine he's there, but I assume he's married, and his wife will let him know we're looking for him."

I knocked on the door. We were met with the smell of baking cookies when the forty-something woman opened the door. She had a quick smile and was wiping her hands on a dishtowel.

"Can I help you?"

Jill took the lead. "We're from the National Park Service, and we'd like to talk to the ranger."

The woman pointed across the parking lot. "Chris is the one in the Smokey Bear hat, holding the clipboard."

We thanked her and edged past the line of boys and adult leaders waiting to speak to the ranger. He was also forty-something and wore a red scout t-shirt and green pants. Everything about him looked comfortable and easygoing, from his smile to his well-worn clothing. We waited until he finished a discussion with a scoutmaster, then stepped forward.

"Could we have a moment of your time?" I asked.

He looked at us, our badges, and weapons, then turned back to the crowd.

"Is there anyone else who doesn't know which cabin they're assigned to or how to find it?"

A boy's voice in the back yelled, "When's the trading post open?"

"Three o'clock," he replied. He held out his clipboard, indicating a sidewalk that ran alongside the building behind him. He unlocked a door and held it open for us.

"I'm Chris Locker, the ranger. How can I help you?"

Jill and I introduced ourselves, and we shook his hand. "I assume you heard about the couple who disappeared upstream on Friday."

"Yeah. That's pretty much every ranger's nightmare."

"We recovered the man's body yesterday just south of the railroad bridge, but the woman is still missing," I explained, not wanting to get into greater detail about the recovery and apparent murder. "Have you seen any of their gear float past, or did you see a boat unload the woman somewhere?"

Chris' eyes flickered with understanding. "You think the woman is alive and someone rescued her."

Jill shook her head. "Please don't share this information, but it appears the woman was kidnapped. We hope to find someone who saw her in a boat and can describe her captors and their vehicle."

Chris leaned his hip against a cooler under a sign with prices for ice cream treats. Other signs displayed the prices for candy, soda pop, uniform patches, and camp souvenirs.

He nodded toward the door. "Unlike this mayhem, it's usually quiet around here during the week. I don't spend a lot of time looking at the river. I'm mostly repairing broken cabin fixtures, restocking woodpiles, and doing bookkeeping. I even get a day a week off to spend with my wife."

Jill smiled. "That's important."

"To answer your question, no, I didn't notice anyone going by with a kidnapped woman in a boat. There's a canoe launch here, but there's not anywhere someone could come in with a boat trailer and pull their boat out of the water."

"Have you recovered any life jackets or paddles with the Taylors Falls outfitter's logo?" I asked.

Chris shook his head. "I haven't, but I don't spend a lot of time down by the river."

Jill looked at a yellowed camp map pinned to the wall. "How big is the camp?"

"The property is 260 acres, but only 60 acres are cleared for camping along the river. A lot of it is the 150-foot bluffs you drove down. We can accommodate 160 cabin campers at a time, plus more tent campers. All the cabins are full May through October and weekends over the winter."

"I camped here back in the day. I recall quite a bit of wild acreage beyond the camping areas."

Chris nodded. "There's a lot of undeveloped land, especially north of the

151

cabins. Some of it gets used for presentations and ceremonies, but a lot of it is just hiking trails or thickets."

"Have you patrolled all of it recently?" Jill asked.

Chris laughed. "I hardly have enough time to do maintenance during the summer, and it's not accessible by vehicle. So, no, I haven't 'patrolled' it since I was snowshoeing last winter."

"Have you been contacted by the Secret Service?" Jill asked.

Chris' smile disappeared. "Why would the Secret Service contact me?"

Chris was unaccustomed to lying. I smiled at him. "I think you already know that the President's son will be canoeing the river next week. The Secret Service wants to secure all the river he'll be canoeing and is arranging for backup extraction points in case they feel uncomfortable with O'Brien State Park."

"That's interesting."

"We heard there were places donated to the scouts when the National Scenic Riverway was established, and development got restricted along the riverbanks."

"They're not really houses, just old cabins that are boarded up."

"Do they have driveway access?" I asked.

"They did have driveways, but we chained the accesses, and they're overgrown with brush and trees now. You'd need a brush hog or chainsaw to open them up."

"When did you last check them?"

"As I said, I was up there last winter. They're still there, although they're in tough shape. One of the roofs collapsed, and the other two are close to that."

"Did you tell the Secret Service about them?"

Chris looked at our badges again. "Can I see your IDs?"

Jill and I took out our folders with pictures and National Park Service credentials, identifying us as investigators. Chris looked at them and handed them back. "It's intimidating having people in suits flashing Secret Service IDs at you and swearing you to secrecy under penalty of federal imprisonment."

Jill smiled. "We're not quite as intimidating as the Secret Service?"

Chris shook his head. "You look more like scoutmasters than federal spooks." He paused. "No, I didn't tell them about the cabins. They kind of bulldozed me, and I answered questions, but never really got beyond their script."

"I assume they want to use your canoe launch as an emergency extraction point," I said.

"I think you know I can't answer that question." He paused. "I'll just say that there won't be any campers here the day of the canoe trip, but there will probably be a cop at the end of our access road and a couple people with guns walking the shore."

"Can you take us up to the abandoned cabins?"

Chris glanced at his watch. "It's Thursday, and I've got over a hundred scouts roaming the campground this week. I'm pretty much a one-man show, and I have to stay close to the trading post in case there's an emergency."

Jill looked at the camp map. "Can we walk there ourselves if you show us where they're located?"

Chris looked at our uniforms and thought. "I can take you there tomorrow after the campers are settled in."

Jill stared into his eyes. "A woman's been kidnapped, and we don't want to wait a day wondering if the kidnappers are holding her in one of the cabins. They sound like a perfect place to stash someone you don't want to be found."

"There's no water or power out there."

Jill nodded. "We didn't say she'd be alive."

Chris' eyes went wide, and he pulled off his Smokey Bear hat. He ran his fingers through his thinning blond hair. "Let me talk to Karen, my wife. She's covered the trading post when I've been sick."

He led us out of the trading post and locked the building behind us. Jill and I stood in the parking lot, watching dozens of scouts gather into troops and walk off different trails to their assigned cabins and campsites.

Jill swatted a mosquito that landed on her neck. "Do we still have bug repellent in the trunk?"

I led her to the rental car and got out bottles of sunscreen and bug repellent. We doped-up our exposed skin. I took my Minnesota Twins cap out and handed Jill her broad-brimmed floppy hat.

"Put bug repellent on your ankles and pants cuffs. The river valley is noted as a deer tick haven, and many carry Lyme disease."

Jill squirted bug repellent in her hand and rubbed it on her socks. "How do you know things like that?"

"The same way I know about the poison ivy experience."

Chris returned, wearing long sleeves and a floppy hat that covered his neck. "Can I have a squirt of your bug juice?"

He wiped it on his hands, neck, face, and ankles. When he handed the bottle back, he checked our ankle-high hiking boots. "You guys look like you're ready for the backcountry. The Secret Service guys looked disturbed because they were getting dust on their shoes in the gravel parking lot."

I took three water bottles out of the trunk and handed one each to Chris and Jill. "Water probably isn't the big deal it was when we were hiking in northern Arizona, but we might as well be prepared."

Chris tipped his bottle toward me. "Be prepared. The scout motto. How far did you make it?"

I knew he meant scout rank. "I'm an Eagle Scout and a member of the Order of the Arrow. This trail takes us past the ceremony ring, right?"

"Yes. Past there, I don't maintain the trails. I've had a couple troops who've spent their weekends clearing and working on the trails, but there's no regular maintenance. Be careful where you step."

"Rattlesnakes?" Jill asked.

"There aren't any rattlesnakes this far north. You're more likely to twist an ankle on a rock or tree root." Chris paused. "There's some poison ivy further north."

"Doug told me, 'leaves of three, let it be.'"

"That's mostly true, but there are also wild strawberries and trillium here. I'll point out the poison ivy when I see it."

We walked a trail marked as the route to three cabins. "It's going to be crazy up here where the boys are setting up, but we'll be past the cabins in ten minutes."

In a short time, the noise of the scouts was behind us, and the only sounds were chirping birds, croaking frogs, and the sound of our boots on the trail.

I felt embarrassed when the buzz of my cellphone broke the silence. I was tempted to turn it off, then remembered the numerous people who'd chastised me earlier.

The caller ID said FBI. "Fletcher."

"You demanded to be kept in the information loop. I'm with the kidnapped woman's father. I've got my electronics guys working with the cellphone the kidnappers sent to him. We'll be able to listen and record when they call back. I've got other people in a van who are ready to get the number off the incoming call and will likely be able to tell us which cell tower is picking up the outgoing call within a minute. In five minutes, if the call lasts that long, they'll be able to triangulate towers and get us within a few houses of the caller."

"Great. How about their demand for the program?"

"That was a little tougher. We had to get the head of the department involved. As you know, that means the potential for a leak. She suggested we use a program they'd developed for an earlier generation of planes. Their company didn't get the contract, but they have a genuine avionics program that should pass a quick sniff test when the kidnappers download it. They're working on a virus they can slip into it, causing a time delay. After a couple hours, the virus will infect the hard drive of any computer that downloads it, sending off pings, like sonar so that the users can be traced. It also leaves a back door open, allowing us to see what they have on their drives and opening the opportunity to corrupt their files slowly. In a week, they won't be able to access anything they have, and every email they send will contain a virus for the recipient."

I stepped across a small brook and nearly wiped out on the wet clay on the other side. "I don't know what all that means, but it sounds impressive."

"It sounds like you're walking. What are you up to?"

"Jill and I are walking with a scout camp ranger to some abandoned cabins. He hasn't been near them since winter, and they seem like a perfect, secluded spot to hide a kidnapped woman. There's no road access, no power, and nobody goes near them except for an occasionally lost scout."

"Interesting. Let me know if you find anything."

"Maggie, I assume you don't know anything more about the exchange of the woman."

"I spoke with her father, but he's had only one call, and they only said they'd release her in some public place once they verify the program."

I ended the call and saw that I was lagging behind Jill and the ranger. I caught up, and Jill looked at me like I'd committed a sin by answering the phone. "Who was it?"

"Maggie, the FBI agent. They're with the father and making plans to hand over the program the kidnapper's demanded."

"I don't like this. If they wanted money, I could see how there'd be an exchange so we could see her before handing over the cash. This electronic stuff is too…theoretical. They hold all the cards and the woman, and we have to trust that they'll release her."

"Welcome to twenty-first-century kidnapping."

Chapter Eleven

The cabin was moss-covered and nearly invisible in the forest, except for the straight lines and square corners that contrasted with the leaning and twisting trees and brush. As expected, the roof sagged but was still intact. I grabbed Chris' shoulder to stop him from marching up to the front door.

"Someone has walked this path recently," I whispered.

"I'm not surprised. The scouts have unstructured time, and they wander all over, climbing the bluffs and exploring the trails. It's part of scout camping."

"We're going to approach slowly with you following me. Jill, go to the back but keep your head below the level of the windows."

Chris looked at me like I'd gone mad when I pulled my pistol. "The plywood over the door is loose. There might be a kid inside there."

I nodded and showed him that I didn't have my finger on the trigger, but alongside the trigger guard. "This isn't my first house entry. I used to be a St. Paul cop."

Chris relaxed and looked at Jill, who was sneaking quietly around the side of the house with her Glock in her hand. "Her too?"

"No, she grew up carrying a gun to school in South Dakota, and she's a seasoned ranger who's been in a couple shootouts. She's not going to shoot anyone by accident."

Chris unclipped a small flashlight from his belt. "You're going to need this. There's no electricity, and the windows are boarded up."

The wooden steps sagged under my weight. The plywood door covering was moss-coated and soggy. The sheet flexed when I pulled on it, and a couple of nails creaked. Anyone inside now knew someone was coming. The flashlight beam was weak and small compared to the tactical flashlights cops carried. The light flashed around an empty room that smelled of mildew and mold. Something fluttered in the attic, and I heard wings beating until the bird or bat found an opening and escaped. Every room was empty. The kitchen counter was made of linoleum that curled along the edges. A hand pump was mounted over a small sink. There were electrical outlets and porcelain light fixtures, which meant electricity had been here once upon a time.

Like the living room and kitchen, the bedrooms were empty. The floor felt soggy under my feet. Above me, there was a large water stain on the ceiling, speaking of the roof's condition. I heard a whisper of cloth behind me and spun around. Chris had walked into the living room, and I scared him when I turned.

"Sorry," he said, putting his hands up. "I was afraid you'd fall through the floor."

The single-story building had only a crawlspace underneath, not a basement. I checked the circumference of the cabin and found the only crawlspace access had been nailed shut and was secure.

Jill followed me back to the front. "Nothing?"

"Birds in the attic." I turned to Chris. "On to the next one."

We followed trails that got narrower and more overgrown. Chris stopped on the edge of a clearing and motioned for Jill. He pointed to waxy, dark green leaves on the forest floor. "That's poison ivy."

She nodded, and we went on.

Fifteen minutes later, we were walking single file down an overgrown path with leaves brushing against us on both sides. Mosquitoes boiled out of the brush as we passed and buzzed around our heads. I was tempted to swat at them, but the repellent was effectively keeping them from landing on me or biting. Chris led the way, his gait easy and he took long steps that had me struggling to keep up in the rear while scanning the underbrush for signs of crossing trails or anything that looked out of place. Overhanging ferns hid a portion of the trail and the tree root that sent me sprawling.

Jill heard me fall. She looked over her shoulder, then stopped, watching me stand up. "Are you okay?"

I brushed the moist dirt off my hands and the knees of my uniform pants. "I'm fine."

A smirk crept onto Jill's face. "What's the matter, did the Eagle Scout bruise his ego?"

Chris stopped, watching our exchange. I put on my confident face. "Just a hidden root. No big deal."

We set off again at the same challenging pace. I lifted my feet higher and kept my eyes on the trail instead of the passing forest.

Chris stopped and raised his hand. "Here's the one with the collapsed roof," he whispered, taking my approach of the first cabin to heart. He stepped aside and let me lead.

This cabin had a narrow porch, and behind it, the river sparkled through a few breaks in the leaves. I could envision someone building this and clearing the brush away to have a view of the river from their porch. It made me nostalgic to think about someone's dream cabin being bought up by the government when the St. Croix had been designated a scenic riverway. The owners had apparently gifted their property to the scouts rather than let the federal government acquire it through eminent domain proceedings.

I motioned for Jill to go around the side and gave Chris a hand signal that I hoped made it clear he wouldn't follow me into the house. The wooden steps were more than soggy, and one of the porch boards had broken under the weight of some previous explorer. I chose not to dwell on that after reasoning that I probably weighed at least fifty pounds more than the average scout.

The roof collapse had pushed down the ceiling in the one-room structure. There was a cast iron stove in what had probably been a kitchen area, and wooden bunkbed frames were built into one wall. There was nothing to be discovered by walking into the room except flooring that might not support my weight. I backed out and called Jill's name.

We met at the bottom step. "Where's the next cabin, Chris?"

"I think these were platted at five-acre lots, so it's probably less than a hundred yards ahead."

"Is it in the same shape as this one?"

"It's newer, and the roof is still intact."

I looked at the porch I'd just crossed. "Has the scout council ever considered tearing these down?"

Chris shook his head. "There's no money to do it, and there's no way to get demolition equipment back here."

"Maybe you should burn them down next winter?"

"Do you think the mildewed wood would burn?"

"With enough fuel oil…"

Chris smiled. "Let me know when you'd like to carry five or ten gallons of fuel oil out here. I'll give you a box of matches."

We walked the trail until it disappeared under the ferns and low bushes. We'd gone nearly a hundred yards when Chris stopped abruptly. I looked over his shoulder, expecting to see the last cabin, but all that was ahead of us was a dense forest.

He pointed toward the river. "Someone's been through here recently."

I stepped next to him and looked where he was pointing. Whatever he saw was escaping me.

He waved me on a few more yards, then he squatted down and held up a fern. "Someone came through here. The plants are crushed, and a few ferns are broken."

Jill was beside me, listening to Chris whisper. She looked in the direction he was pointing. "It's subtle, but I see a trail coming up from the river."

"Do you have a cellphone?" I whispered to Chris.

He pulled a near-military-grade flip phone out of his pocket and held it up.

"Wait here. If someone starts shooting, or if we're not back in ten minutes, dial 911 and get back to the main trail."

Chris shook his head. "We're only a little way from the north edge of the scout camp. There's a clearing ahead and a place where I can get a 4X4 pickup down here."

I looked at Jill. "If there's any place along here I'd stash someone I'd kidnapped, it'd be here. Are you ready for this?"

She looked taunt, like a lioness ready to spring. "Let's do it," she whispered.

I led us down the faint trail until the house was in sight. Well concealed, I stopped for a minute to listen and watch. There was no activity and no noise, except for the chirping birds and the buzzing mosquitoes. I looked at Jill. Her hat was ringed with sweat, and a bead had trickled past her ear. Her shirt was damp, and she was scraped, and her pants dirty.

"The same approach as the last cabin, only be more cautious."

She nodded and skirted around the cabin. I went to the side, so I wasn't approaching the door head-on. The top step was recently broken, so I took a long step up to the narrow porch, which groaned under my weight. Something scraped inside.

I felt the cellphone in my pocket and briefly considered backing away and calling the FBI. I blew off that thought, partly out of the fear of being embarrassed if the sound I'd heard was a raccoon or some other critter. Before I took another step, muffled noise from inside sounded human.

I sidled up to the door. The plywood had been pulled off, and the door was slightly ajar. I tried to guess what the interior layout was, but there weren't any clues, except for the boarded-up window next to the door. I'd seen two windows on the side, so there was a chance there were bedrooms rather than the one open room in the previous cabin.

Weighing the option of easing the door open and tipping off someone inside against kicking the door and bursting through it, I decided the quick entry might give me a second to surprise whoever was inside.

My foot hit the door and it crashed open as I flew through the frame, dodging to the right so I wouldn't be silhouetted with the light behind me. The folly of the whole plan struck me when I realized how dark the room was and how weak the flashlight beam was.

The living room I'd entered was empty with spongy wall-to-wall carpeting under my feet. To the right was a door into an empty kitchen. The cupboard doors were open, exposing dusty shelves. The countertop was Formica, and there was a faucet on the sink, hinting at a time when there'd been an electrical pump.

I backed out of the kitchen and eased toward three closed doors. My eyes were adjusting to the dim light filtering around the boards over the windows. I reasoned that the right door backed up against the kitchen, and the builders probably economized on the pipe by putting the kitchen and bathroom back-to-back on the same wall. I turned the knob and opened the door, causing the hinges to creak. Something shuffled on the floor behind the door across the hallway.

I verified nothing was in the bathroom except the stubs of cast iron pipes and holes where copper pipes had probably been torn out when metal prices had spiked.

There wasn't enough space to get my leg up to kick the bedroom door, and my knee screamed at me for using that foot on the front door. I put my back against the wall.

"Police! Come out with your hands up!"

There was no hail of gunfire, just more scraping and muffled noises that sounded human. I pushed the door open and jumped back. Again, there was no gunfire, but the scraping was more urgent, and the muffled noises frantic. I spun around the doorframe, holding the pistol in front of me and sweeping it from side to side.

"Jill! Get in here!"

Jill flew through the door, leading with her gun when I tore the duct tape from the nude woman's wrists. I'd already ripped it off her mouth, making her parched lips bleed. She lay sobbing, not saying anything. Every inch of her body was covered with welts from mosquito bites, making me reflect on Cheryl's admonition to use insect repellent, or the mosquitoes would suck me dry. A swollen wood tick was attached behind her left ear, gray and nearly as big as a dime.

I tore at the tape around her ankles while Jill holstered her gun and pulled the water bottle out of her cargo pants pocket. Jill helped the woman sit up, and I untucked and unbuttoned my shirt. With my shirt over her shoulders, the woman began to shake. Jill held the water bottle to her mouth, but her lips and tongue were so swollen that most of it seemed to dribble out of the corners of her mouth.

I left Jill with my water bottle and walked through the house as I punched in Maggie Steller's phone number. As the phone rang, I yelled, "Chris! Dial 911 and figure out how to get an ambulance down here!"

"Fletcher, now's not a good time. I'll…" Maggie whispered.

"We found the woman. She's alive."

"What woman?"

"The kidnapped woman."

"Wait. What? Where are you?"

Chris came running through the underbrush with his phone to his ear. "What do I tell them?"

"Tell them we've got an exposure victim who's badly dehydrated and covered in mosquito bites." I put my phone back to my ear. "Did you hear that?"

"Yes but, where are you?"

"Wisconsin. At the scout camp. We searched cabins in the camp's remote parts and found the woman bound and lying on the floor. She's in bad shape, but she's alive."

"Have you asked her what happened?"

"Maggie, aren't you listening? She's in bad shape. She's covered in bug bites and it looks like she hasn't had water for several days. Her lips and tongue are swollen, so she can't talk or even take a swallow out of a water bottle."

"Okay, I get the picture. We're on the phone with the kidnappers. Stay with the woman wherever the ambulance takes her. Don't identify her to anyone. We want the kidnappers to think we're at their mercy."

"They'll figure it out when they come to pick her up."

There was a pause. "Doug, does it look like they were coming back to get her?"

I pulled off my Twins cap as the reality of Maggie's words hit me. I looked at the sun's reflection off the river and thought about man's inhumanity to man.

"Are you still there, Doug?"

"Yeah."

"Stay with her and keep her incognito. Call me as soon as you get her to a hospital, and I'll dispatch a security detail."

"No, Maggie. Sending in an army of FBI agents will set off alarms, and someone's going to call a television station. Jill and I will stay with her. As far as anyone at the hospital will know, we're just a couple rangers, helping a stranded hiker."

"Good thinking. I hate to say this, but we're not going to tell her father right now. He might blow the whole thing before we track down the kidnappers. Oh, shit. The park superintendent is her aunt. Don't tell her either."

"Maggie, we're professional federal agents. We're not going to blow your operation, and we're not going to leak the information. Trust me."

"All right, but if you burn me…"

"I won't."

"You have a reputation…"

"I have a reputation for doing the right thing for the right reasons. The only time I've burned the FBI is when we've been kept outside the information loop. I'm your partner in this. Okay?"

"And Jill?"

"Jill's also a professional. You won't have any problems with us."

"Okay. Okay. Call me from the hospital so I know where you are."

Chris was standing next to me. "They're not going to be able to get the ambulance down the cliff. Can the woman walk up on her own?"

I put my hand on his arm. "I'm going to tell you something in the strictest confidence. If you thought the Secret Service agents were scary, this is going to be a whole level higher."

"Okay."

"We have to get the woman out of here and to a hospital, but we need to do it quietly. You don't know who she is, right?"

"She's the woman who was kidnapped."

I shook my head. "If anyone asks, and I doubt they will, you'll tell them that we found a hiker in the woods who'd been separated from her group." I weighed telling him more, and then something unexpected jumped to mind. "Swear on your scout's honor that you won't divulge what I'm about to tell you until you hear it on the news."

"C'mon. We're adults."

"A scout's honor means something to us, right?"

Chris nodded. "Okay. You've got it."

"The FBI is negotiating with the kidnappers right now. The kidnappers can not know that we've found the woman, or the FBI sting will collapse, and they'll get away. So, Jill will ride to the hospital in the ambulance. You and I will follow. The woman in there is delusional from dehydration and exposure. We don't know her name or exactly how she got here."

"You've got to be joking."

"I'm serious, and if you leak this or ruin the FBI operation, there will be federal consequences."

"Got it."

"Can you get your pickup down here?"

"Sure, but it'll take me an hour to make the trip. The sheriff can have…"

"I don't want the sheriff involved. Can your wife drive the pickup?"

"Yes."

"Call her."

"She doesn't like driving down the bluff at the camp, and this is…."

"Do you want to carry that woman up the hill over your shoulder?"

Chris pondered the options for a millisecond and pulled out his phone. He turned his back to me, but I could tell he was working on a hard sell.

He folded his phone. "She's not happy, but she'll be here in ten or fifteen minutes."

"Will you jog up the hill and ask the EMTs to come down with their bags?"

Chris trotted off through the underbrush. I judged him to be only a couple of years younger than me, but his job left him in much better shape.

"Doug."

I walked back into the cabin and was surprised to see Jill sitting on the floor, wearing only her sports bra. Mosquitoes swarmed around her. I realized she'd taken off her shirt and covered the woman's hips because my shirt wasn't quite long enough to meet Jill's sense of modesty. "What do you need?"

"She can't swallow. She needs an IV."

"Chris just ran up the hill to get the EMTs. His wife will be here with the pickup truck in maybe fifteen minutes."

"The pickup?"

"Chris said the ambulance is too wide to drive down the hill. She's coming in their four-wheel-drive pickup."

Our patient's eyes were closed, and she was lying on her back. Her breathing was raspy, and all the mosquito bites made it look like she had the measles. She said something, but her swollen tongue made it so garbled I couldn't discern her words. I looked at Jill, who shrugged.

Jill laid next to the woman on the floor and stroked her hair. "There's an ambulance on the way."

The woman said something, this time opening her eyes and speaking emphatically.

Her inflection made it sound like she was asking a question.

Jill's eyes showed recognition. "We'll check on him when we get you to the hospital. Okay?"

The woman closed her eyes. Jill mouthed, "husband."

I nodded toward the door, but Jill shook her head, picking up the woman's hand instead.

"I need you to ride in the ambulance with her." I weighed my words carefully, trying to tell Jill what was going on without upsetting our patient. "I spoke with Maggie. Her plan is going forward, and we're going to stay at the hospital until we're relieved." I patted my holster.

"Have you called Cheryl yet?"

I shook my head emphatically and put up my hands. "Maggie asked me to hold off until…other things were resolved."

Jill didn't like that answer but didn't reach for her phone. I nodded toward the door, and again, she shook her head and squeezed our patient's hand.

I heard the low-gear whine of the pickup. I walked to the barbed wire fence, marking the end of the scout camp, and watched as the pickup, driven by the ranger, eased down a narrow driveway carved into the hillside. This driveway made the scout driveway look like a four-lane interstate highway.

They got to the bottom of the hill and bounced across what was probably an old, rutted driveway to where I was standing. Two EMTs

174

sitting in the back of the truck jumped over the fenders and grabbed their bags. I led them to the cabin, and Jill stepped back to let them treat the patient.

I heard one of them speaking into a radio, reporting vital signs, and his observations. I knew that her blood pressure was dangerously low, and her pulse too high due to dehydration.

"I've got a vein," one of them said as the other lifted an IV bag.

I took Jill's hand, pulled her to her feet, and led her outside the cabin. "Maggie was on the phone with the kidnappers when I called her. She wants us to protect the woman without making a fuss that someone in the hospital will report as suspicious. We talked about an FBI team, but that might make the news, and she needs to keep the rescue off the news until they catch the kidnappers."

"Why don't they just set up here and catch them when they come back to make the exchange?"

"They're not coming back."

"But..." Jill's eyes filled with tears as the reality of my words hit. "They were going to leave her here?" she hissed.

I shrugged. "They might've provided her location at some point. Or they might've just left her. Either way, they aren't coming back."

"So, what are we supposed to do?"

"She's Jane Doe. She was lost in the park, apparently separated from her hiking group. We're the concerned park rangers who aren't going to raise anyone's eyebrows." I looked at Jill's torso. "Well, not if you put your shirt back on."

Jill looked down and quickly crossed her arms across her chest. "Geez, the EMTs…"

"Trust me. They've seen it all."

"Yeah, well, they haven't seen 'my all.'"

Chris and his wife trotted down what was becoming a trail trampled through the undergrowth. He had his arm over her shoulder, and she looked shellshocked. She looked at Jill's bra and mosquito-bitten torso. "What happened to your shirt?"

"I put it on the woman inside. She was naked when we found her."

Chris's wife turned to him. "Be a gentleman and give her your shirt. You don't want her running around in her underwear."

Chris, who had run up and then down the hill, stripped off his sweat-stained t-shirt and handed it to Jill. She pulled it over her head and promised to return it. It hung on her like a nightshirt, and she gave me a quick look that said it was a bit gamy.

One of the EMTs stuck his head out the cabin door. "There's a backboard in the pickup. Could one of you bring it in here?"

Four of us carried our patient to the pickup with Chris' wife carrying the IV bag as high as she could reach. We made the precarious ride back up the hill with what seemed like one tire hanging over the edge.

With the patient loaded into the ambulance, the EMT in the back looked between us. "Can one of you provide her information?"

I pushed Jill forward. "My partner will ride with you. Where are you taking her?"

"St. Paul is the nearest trauma hospital."

"Nothing in Hudson?"

The EMT closed the back of the ambulance. "Not Hudson. Stillwater has an ER, but they're not a level one trauma center."

"Take her to Stillwater."

The EMT frowned. "I think…"

I held up my badge. "Stillwater. Understood?"

"She's…"

"She's dehydrated and mosquito-bitten. No gunshot wounds. No broken bones. No major trauma. Stillwater."

They drove off with the siren wailing. I looked at Chris. "Can I ride back to the camp with you, so I can retrieve my rental car?"

I offered my hand to Chris' wife. "We got a little rushed and never got introduced. I'm Doug Fletcher."

Chris' wife smiled. "Camp rangers aren't known for their etiquette. I'm Karen."

"Did Chris talk to you about our 'situation?'"

Karen nodded. "Jane Doe got separated from her hiking group."

I smiled. "Thank you both. I think we saved that woman's life today."

Karen glanced at me. "I don't think of the National Park Service Rangers as lifesavers. I mean, you guys do first aid and stuff, but…wow, this is something."

"Tell your grandchildren about it, but please keep it quiet, at least until you hear about this rescue on the news."

"You think this will be on the news?"

"I guarantee it."

Chapter Twelve

Jill was in the ER waiting room. At some point, she'd swapped Chris' shirt for her own. "What's going on?"

"The doctor kicked me out. She was going to do a rape kit because she found some bruises, and the patient came in naked."

"Is she still Jane Doe?"

"So far. No one is happy about that, but the patient can't provide any information to them. At least not yet."

I stood up. "C'mon, we're going to talk to the doctor and nurses."

Jill got up and followed me. "Are you being overly dramatic?"

"Not at all."

I stopped at the ER desk, and a woman looked up. "Can I help you?"

"I need to speak with the doctor and nurses who are treating Jane Doe."

"Are you her family?"

I unfolded my credentials and flashed them quickly, hoping she didn't have time to read them. "I'm a federal agent and need to speak with the doctor right now."

"She's treating…"

I sat on the counter. "I'll wait here."

"The waiting room is…"

"We're waiting here and speaking with the doctor as soon as she walks out of a treatment room."

The doctor didn't appear for fifteen minutes and seemed pre-occupied until I stepped directly into her path. She looked up. "Excuse me."

"We need to have an immediate discussion."

"I'm not accustomed to irate demands from random people who walk into my ER."

"Jane Doe is under our protection, and we need to talk about her."

That piqued the doctor's curiosity. "Protection?"

"She's in protective custody. Where can we talk with you and her nurse privately?"

The doctor glanced at our badges and holsters, then nodded toward a door at the end of the hallway. "I'll get Belle."

The doctor left, and I leaned close to Jill. "Go sit with our patient."

"Yes sir, Mr. National Park Service Inspector, sir."

I looked at the ceiling. "Please keep an eye on our patient."

A smiled flickered. "Better. Try that approach first next time."

I kissed her. "I'll try to remember."

The doctor and a nurse, both in scrubs, came around a corner just as I kissed Jill.

Jill smiled. "It's okay. We're federal cops."

180

The look on the doctor's face was priceless. She led me to a family consultation room and closed the door. "What's up?" The doctor's nametag said, "Holbrook M.D."

"Our Jane Doe needs to remain anonymous for the time being."

Dr. Holbrook glared at me. "That's it? You dragged me in here to remind me about the HIPAA rules?" She reached for the doorknob.

"Hear me out…" I remembered Jill's admonition. "Please sit down for a moment."

The nurse sat, but Dr. Holbrook remained standing. "What are you trying to pull? You strut in here like you own the place and start dictating to us."

I put up my hands. "I have to rely on your discretion. The woman in the exam room has suffered extreme physical and emotional trauma. I can't discuss the details, but her safety depends on your cooperation."

Holbrook continued to glare at me but sat. "I saw the adhesive residue and bruising on her wrists and ankles. The EMTs reported that she was naked when they found her, so I ran a rape kit. What do you know that I don't?"

"We're protecting her while the FBI completes a sting. If word leaks out that she's been found, the people will escape, who tied her up and left her for dead."

Holbrook looked at my badge. "This is pretty far fetched. You're a National Park Service ranger, not an FBI agent."

I took out my laminated credentials and passed them to her. "My partner and I are National Park Service investigators from Texas coordinating with the FBI. The woman was kidnapped from the St. Croix last Friday, and we've been searching for her for a week. We found her husband in the river yesterday with an anchor tied around his ankles."

Holbrook's eyes softened, and she handed the ID wallet to the nurse. "Does she know her husband is dead?"

"Not yet. In my judgment, she wasn't ready to receive that news."

"It's nice to know a National Park Service ranger has the compassion not to drop a bombshell on a delirious woman."

I pulled out my wallet, dug out my credentials, identifying me as a St. Paul police retiree, and handed them to the doctor. "Does it help to know I was a 'real' cop for seventeen years before I became a sworn federal agent?"

Holbrook fingered my ID and handed it back to me. "So, what do you want from us?"

"That young woman has to remain unnamed. Better yet if no one even knows she's here. That's why you've got two National Park Service investigators sitting with her instead of a team of FBI agents or U.S. Marshals. We need this off the radar and out of the headlines for the next twenty-four hours."

The nurse, whose nametag said she was Annabelle Z. RN, spoke up. "I heard something about a body being recovered from the river yesterday. There wasn't anything on the news."

Holbrook listened and turned to me. "Who recovered the body?"

"I was in a canoe and found it. I went out with the sheriff department's divers to make the recovery. They spent twenty minutes scouring the bottom after the recovery to see if this woman was there, too."

"You saw her husband's body?"

"I lifted it into the boat."

Holbrook digested that and stood. "I have other patients."

I was going to reach for her arm and decided that might ignite the flickering flame. Instead, I put up my hand. "Will you cooperate?"

Holbrook stared at me for a moment, considering my request. "I want the woman's name. I want to go into her room and say it aloud so that I can connect with her. It'll lower her anxiety and help me bond with her."

I nodded. "But don't put it into your computer system or write it on the whiteboard where you're tracking the ER census. She has to remain Jane Doe."

Holbrook looked at the nurse. "Belle, let's do as he asks...for the time being."

"Thank you. Please hang on for one moment." I took a business card from my wallet and wrote Maggie Steller's cellphone number on the back. "This is the phone number for the FBI special agent who's handling the case. If you have any doubts about my veracity or the need to keep this confidential, please call her."

Holbrook looked at the number with disgust. "This could be anyone's number."

"Then call the Minneapolis FBI office and ask for Special Agent Margaret Steller and tell them you're calling on my behalf. She'll call you back within fifteen minutes from this number."

Holbrook handed the card to Belle. "Call the sheriff's department and ask about a National Park Service ranger named Fletcher."

"The FBI hasn't involved them yet. Please call the FBI directly. The investigator who's in with Jane Doe is Jill Fletcher."

Holbrook took the card, read my name, and smiled. "I assume that's the reason I saw you kissing her in the hallway."

"We're newlyweds, and this is supposed to be our honeymoon."

Belle smiled. "Personally, I'd opt for a quieter honeymoon."

The doctor edged past me and opened the door. "If nothing else, stay out of the way."

I leaned close to the doctor. "Your patient's name is Janet Eastman."

Holbrook raised her eyebrows. "That wasn't so hard, was it?"

* * *

I walked to the exam room and knocked gently on the door before entering. Janet Eastman's eyes were closed. Two IV bags hung next to her bed, and an electronic monitor gave off a reassuring 'beep, beep, beep,' and displayed her pulse and blood pressure. Her complexion appeared pale, and her lips were cracked and peeling. She wore a hospital gown and was covered with a sheet, so all I could see were her shoulders, arms, and face. She was still covered with raised red welts from the mosquito bites.

Jill had changed into her uniform shirt in the bathroom and scratched at the mosquito bites covering her torso. She held out my shirt. "You'll look more professional if you're wearing a shirt."

Janet's eyes popped open when she heard our voices. She looked scared. "Who are you?" she croaked.

"I'm Doug Fletcher. My wife, Jill, has been sitting with you."

Janet's eyes flickered, and it seemed like she relaxed a bit. She looked at the badge on my belt as I tucked and buttoned my shirt.

Jill squeezed Janet's hand. "I told her that we're here to protect her."

Janet's gaze went back to my face. "Where's my husband?"

"I honestly don't know." It wasn't a lie but was undoubtedly a sin of omission. "When did you last see him?"

"What day is it?"

"Thursday."

"We were canoeing…Friday. Two fishermen came to help us when our canoe tipped. One of them..." Janet's eyes closed. I'm sure she would've cried if she had enough fluids to generate tears.

"What did the men look like?"

Jill frowned at me and gave me a tiny headshake as the beeping monitor sped up.

I nodded toward the door, and Jill followed me into the hallway. Belle was on the phone with her hand over the speaker, making sure no one was listening. I hoped she was calling the FBI and not the local television station.

"We need to get descriptions of the attackers to Maggie. That could be valuable if they narrow their search to a small public area when the kidnappers call from a cellphone."

"It seems heartless. She's so..."

Nurse Belle was staring at me when she hung up. She walked to Dr. Holbrook, who was busy on a computer workstation. She whispered something to the doctor that made her look up and search the area.

She got up and walked to Jill and me. "Belle left a message for Agent Steller." Holbrook paused. "I guess you're halfway there. At least, there really is an Agent Steller."

A phone rang at the desk, and one of the women answered, looked surprised, then surveyed the area. She franticly waved when she spotted Holbrook.

Holbrook took the call, all the time watching Jill and me. I took a casual look around the area every few minutes to see if anyone was too interested in seeing two people in National Park Service uniforms standing in the ER. No one seemed to care about us.

The doctor hung up the phone and touched Belle's shoulder. They walked over to us, then made sure no one was within earshot.

"Special Agent Steller wasn't pleased about my call," Holbrook said. "I told her I didn't give a damn whether I pleased her or not, and I was irritated that there were two people who claimed to be from the National Park Service trying to order me around."

The doctor let a person in scrubs push a cart of blood samples past before continuing, "Minus a few expletives, Steller told me you two spoke with the full authority of the FBI. Not acting as you directed would result in being charged with interference in a federal investigation."

Jill tried to hide her smile by pretending to cough.

"Did you agree to work with us?" I asked.

"No. I was going to chew her butt for not calling ahead and *requesting* our cooperation, but she hung up on me."

"Where does that leave us?" I asked.

"We'll play along...for now."

Tones chimed at the desk. Holbrook looked down the hallway. "I've got more important things right now. Like I said before, stay out of the way. We've got an ambulance coming."

Jill leaned close. "Does that mean she's cooperating?"

"She's god in this little world, and I think she wanted to let us know that we've begrudgingly won her compliance." I looked around again, and the only people nearby seemed only interested in preparing for the approaching ambulance. "I'll flip a coin to see who goes for coffee."

Jill shook her head. "I need a bathroom. I'll get coffee on my way back."

I peeked in the exam room. Janet seemed to be resting quietly, so I closed the door and took a chair from the empty exam room next door. When Jill returned with the coffees, I was reading a four-year-old copy of *Field and Stream*.

"Why are you reading a dog-eared magazine?"

"I'm years behind on my strategies for catching big bass."

Jill handed me the paper cup with a plastic lid. "It seems like you'd prefer a strategy from this century."

I got up and gave her the chair. "It doesn't matter. I haven't been fishing since the eighties, and I don't plan on going any time soon."

"Then why read it at all?"

"Someone kept me up half the night, and I'm trying to stay awake."

She hooked one of my belt loops with a finger and pulled me closer. "*I* wasn't the reason you were awake half the night."

"Oh? Was there someone else in bed with us?" I whispered.

"Shh." Jill's dimples showed as she glanced around. "What are we doing?"

"Just hanging out, making sure no one asks our patient's name while trying to stay alert."

"I think we should call Cheryl. Our patient needs to see a friendly face."

"Absolutely not. She'll call her brother, and everything could fall apart. That's why Maggie didn't want to involve any other agencies. She's afraid a leak could get to the news people, and the kidnappers might escape before she can close the trap on them."

"We could explain it to her…"

"And she'd explain it to her brother, who'd explain it to his wife, who'd explain it to their neighbor, who happens to be the channel six news producer's second cousin. The information has to end with us. It's risky enough telling the doctor and nurse."

The ER came alive. Dr. Holbrook and nurses were dressed in protective gowns and face masks as they rushed to the ambulance door. A minute later, the doors flew open as two EMTs pushed in a gurney. Holbrook watched as one of her people took over chest compressions on a pasty obese man. They rushed into an exam room, followed by someone pushing a red cart of supplies.

We heard Holbrook calling out orders as people scrambled in and out of the room. A deputy sheriff walked in and talked to a person at the desk. I pushed the exam room door open and attempted to slip inside unnoticed, but he saw me before we were out of sight. His eyes flashed recognition, having been at the river yesterday, and he approached us.

"Hey, Fletchers. What's up?"

"We have an injured park visitor," I said, pushing Jill into the exam room and kicking myself for not asking the doctor to move Janet Eastman to a private hospital room instead of keeping her in the relatively busy ER.

The deputy frowned. "I heard an ambulance call but didn't realize it was for someone in the park."

"We have a visitor who got separated from her hiking group and got a little messed up. She's going to be okay, but we wanted a doctor to look at her."

The deputy nodded, apparently satisfied with my answer. "There are like four hundred people out looking for that missing woman. I suppose somebody stumbled across your hiker during the search. Lucky for her."

"Yeah, lucky."

He turned to walk away, then stopped. "Did you guys talk to the scout camp rangers?"

"Yeah. They haven't seen anything of the life jackets or canoe paddles."

He nodded, then walked to the desk and struck up a conversation with the woman answering the phones. It seemed surreal to witness their quiet conversation being offset by the frantic orders flying out of the exam room where Dr. Holbrook was trying to save a man's life.

Chapter Thirteen

Jill sat in the room with Janet Eastman, and I sat on a chair in the hallway. Activity associated with the ambulance arrival subsided, and the patient was loaded onto a different ambulance and sent away. The doctor disappeared, and the sense of calmness swept back into the ER. Other patients were brought into exam rooms, and Nurse Belle went from room to room, probably taking histories and gathering information on treatment needs.

Dr. Holbrook walked down the hall with purpose, making eye contact with me. I got up and opened the door to the exam room. Holbrook shook her head and nodded toward a corner. "What have you heard from the FBI?"

"Nothing. I assume their operation to capture the kidnappers is ongoing. Why, is someone asking questions?"

"Not that I know about. I was curious." She looked around furtively. "I've ordered a clear liquid meal for Jane Doe. I'm going to grab a sandwich. Would you like to join me?"

I tried not to express my surprise. "Sure. Let me warn Jill."

Holbrook led me to the cafeteria, which was nearly empty now in mid-afternoon. The smell of food reminded me I hadn't eaten since breakfast at the Inn. We cruised through the buffet selections of casseroles, a grill where I could've had a burger, then stopped at a salad bar. I loaded a plate with a little lettuce and more generous portions of diced ham, cheese, and croutons. The clerk weighed our salads, and Holbrook waved off my offer to buy, paying for both of us with a card.

"You said you were from Texas, but you have a St. Paul PD card and no southern accent."

"I grew up in St. Paul, where I was a cop. The National Park Service hired me after I retired."

Holbrook looked at me like she expected more as she chewed her salad.

I ate and didn't go on.

"Where did you meet your wife?"

"We worked together in Arizona."

Holbrook waited for more but didn't get it.

"What do you investigate?"

"Primarily deaths on National Park Service property."

Holbrook set her fork down and leaned on her elbows. "Quit being an ass. I'm trying to have a polite conversation, and you're turning it into twenty questions."

"Okay, what's your history?"

"I grew up in Moorhead, go Spuds! and went to UMD. I got into the U of M med school, liked the urgency of being in the ER, did a residency in Rochester, then got hired here."

"Married?"

"Not yet, but my job doesn't leave room for much socializing."

I guessed Dr. Holbrook was in her mid-thirties. "Your biological clock is ticking."

"Yeah, it can tick all it wants. I'm not rushing into a relationship or having a kid without having a partner to help raise it." She paused. "Do you and Jill have kids?"

I shook my head. "We've only been married a year, and our biological clocks have stopped."

"Were you both divorcees?"

"I'm divorced. Jill was married to her job for thirty years."

"I Googled you while we were waiting for the FBI to call back. I wanted to make sure you were the real thing."

I nodded.

Holbrook took out a smartphone and entered a password. She pulled up something and slid her phone across the table. "This is you and Jill, right?"

She'd found a story about our investigation of a Devils Tower fall. I glanced at the headline and slid the phone back. "That was us."

She punched in something else. "Looks like you were involved in a couple investigations in Flagstaff before you moved to Texas."

"I met Jill in Flagstaff."

Holbrook pocketed her phone and finished her salad. She pushed the bowl aside. "You two are the real deal, not some average park rangers."

I didn't respond.

"Listen, Fletcher. I'm concerned about the safety of my patients and staff. You're not here being nice guys who rescued a kidnapping victim. You said you were here to protect her. Are we in danger because she's here? Is that why you're here?"

I picked up my bowl and nested it in Holbrook's. "We think Jane Doe was abandoned by the kidnappers without them ever intending to return to her. There's an outside chance they'd come back to release her, but no one in law enforcement believes that. Kidnap victims are expendable to their kidnappers, and most of them are dead within hours of their capture. However, for her safety, and yours, Jill and I are here until we hear from the FBI that the kidnappers have been caught or have fled."

"I'll take another look at my patient, but if she's hydrated and suffering from nothing else but mosquito bites, she doesn't need to be here."

"Are you saying you're going to release her or telling me to get her out of here for the safety of your patients and staff?"

Holbrook placed her elbows on the table and looked around at the nearly empty cafeteria. No one was close enough to hear us. "You're a little scary to have around. When I read your news clippings, it seems like you're in the middle of a lot of mayhem. I don't need or want that here."

"I've never shot an innocent person."

"That's you. How about the people who may be coming for my patient? Will they be as careful with their gunfire as you?"

I leaned across the table. "No one is coming for her. They don't care if she's dead or alive. My role here is to keep her identity hidden until after the arrest of the kidnappers. I'm protecting her from the news media, not the kidnappers."

Holbrook leaned back and digested my words. She reached out and picked up our bowls, then stood. "C'mon."

I followed her out of the cafeteria and down the hallway. She stopped in an empty area near the gift shop. "Okay. The ER is too busy, with too many people coming and going. The surgical floors empty out on the weekends. I'll have Belle find an open bed at the end of a hallway, and I'll transfer Jane Doe there for observation."

"That means another group of nurses and admin people will know she's here."

"She's moving as Jane Doe. That'll raise some eyebrows, but not any alarms. I'll distract the rest of the ER staff while Belle moves her. I think we can pull this off without anyone becoming suspicious."

"Thank you."

I followed Holbrook into the ER. I went to Janet's room while the doctor went to the desk.

"I spoke with the ER doctor. She's moving Janet to a surgical floor for observation."

Jill got up, and Janet's eyes fluttered open. "They don't want her down here?"

"There's too much traffic down here. They're going to find a quiet room at the end of a hallway."

Janet pushed herself up on one elbow. "You don't have to talk about me like I'm not here."

I smiled. "I'm sorry. You were delirious the last time I saw you. Are you feeling better?"

"I feel fine. If you can find my clothes, I think I'll leave."

Jill sat on the edge of the bed. "Tell me what you remember about arriving here."

"I imagine you guys brought me here. You're rangers, right?"

"Yes, we're rangers, but we didn't bring you to the hospital. What's the last thing you remember?"

Janet stared at Jill, then at me. "I...we were on the river. Something happened to our canoe, and it tipped." She paused, and I wondered if she was struggling to remember or if the memories were too troubling to vocalize. She looked at me. "Where's Dave?"

"We still don't know where he is, and the doctor wants to keep you under observation for a day until she's sure you don't have some other medical conditions."

Janet looked around the room. "Hand me the phone. I'll call my dad, and he can pick me up." She reached toward the tray table that was just out of reach. "Are we in St. Paul?"

Jill looked at me, then took Janet's hand. "You're not in St. Paul, and you can't call your father right now."

"What's going on?"

"We," Jill stalled, not sure what to say.

I went for limited truth. "You were kidnapped, and we've been assigned to protect you while the kidnappers are being pursued."

Janet looked at our uniforms and the National Park Service patches on our shoulders. "You're rangers. Why would you protect me?"

I put my hand on my holster. "We're National Park Service investigators. We found you in a remote cabin and got you here."

Janet processed the information. "A cabin in the woods."

Jill picked up Janet's hand. "Describe the men who took you there."

"They had a boat, and...they ripped off my bathing suit top and stuffed it into my mouth."

"Describe them."

"They weren't old, and they had tattoos. They were fishing and wore caps."

I sat in the chair. "Did they have brown hair, blonde hair, black hair? Did they have facial hair or mustaches?"

"One guy had brown hair and wore a red cap that had a big letter C on it. The other one was kind of sun-bleached. He had a black cap with a strange logo I didn't know. They both had a couple days of beard."

"Did they use names?"

Janet closed her eyes. "Jimbo. The blonde guy was Jimbo. The other one yelled at him and told him not to…" She shuddered and pulled her knees up, clutching them.

Jill looked at me with the saddest expression I'd ever seen on her face. She clenched her jaw, then looked up into the corner of the room.

The exam room door opened abruptly. I reached for my Sig, and Jill jumped up and put herself between Janet and the door.

"Move time," Belle said. She froze when she realized I had my weapon pointed at her feet, and Jill was clutching Janet protectively. "Oh. Sorry."

I holstered the Sig. Janet shuddered as she reached out and pulled Jill close.

"We've got a second-floor room at the end of the hallway. All the nearby rooms are empty."

I stepped into the hallway and confirmed that no one was paying us any attention. "Sounds great."

Belle lowered the head of the hospital bed. Jill pulled the sheet up to Janet's chin.

"Which way are we going, Belle?"

"We'll go past the center island and take a right to the elevators."

I nodded. "I'll lead the way. Jill is going to walk with her back to the desk so no one can see Janet's face."

* * *

The hospital room was empty and bare. Belle wheeled the bed in, and I opened the rollup blind to a street view in front of the hospital. When Janet was settled, I followed Belle into the hallway.

"I'm sorry I scared you downstairs."

Belle didn't meet my eyes, staring instead at the window in the hallway. "I guess I didn't realize how…serious you two were. Dr. Holbrook said you were real cops, but…"

"Please don't tell anyone about any of this. Okay?"

"No problem," Belle said, then paused. "You know there are HIPAA laws, and people get fired for revealing patients' names or medical information."

"Just the same, thanks."

Belle nodded and walked away.

I was turning to return to the room when my phone trilled. "Fletcher."

"Are you still sitting on Jane Doe?"

I recognized Maggie Steller's voice. "We just moved her to a second-floor room on a half-empty surgical floor. I've got vague descriptions of her abductors."

"Great. It's going down in about an hour. What do the kidnappers look like?"

I gave Maggie the description, and that one was called Jimbo.

"How is the patient?"

"She's perking up. She got some Jell-O and broth, then asked us for her clothes. She's asked twice where her husband is."

"What did you tell her?"

"The truth—that I didn't know where he was."

"Can you keep her under wraps a couple more hours?"

"I don't think that'll be a problem. She's groggy and doesn't have any clothes."

"I'm more concerned about her identity being secure."

"I've got the doctor and nurse on board. Her records list her as Jane Doe."

"Excellent!"

"Maggie, the kidnapper called Jimbo, raped her."

Maggie let out a deep breath. "I suspected that when you said you'd found her naked. I suppose the kidnappers figured she wouldn't be found alive and maybe not for weeks, months, or years."

"I think Jill would like to be along for the arrest. I'm fairly sure she'd shoot the guy."

"If we arrest these guys, they're going to be in prison for a long, long time. A quick death would probably be preferable to whatever they'll endure in maximum-security."

"I know that, but I'm sure Jill wanted me to convey that request."

"Tell you what. You tell her that I'll do my best to restrain myself, but I might not be successful."

I laughed. "I'm sure she'll appreciate the sentiment."

I walked into the room and was surprised to see Janet looking out the window, the back of her hospital gown exposing a sliver of her butt. Jill stood beside her, facing the door.

"I heard you talking to someone in the hall."

"Maggie says this may wrap up in a couple hours."

Janet turned. "Then what happens?"

"Then, we call your parents and Aunt Cheryl to tell them you're okay."

"They don't know?"

I shook my head. "What's happening is very delicate, and if someone let slip that you were safe, the kidnappers might get away."

"But..."

"Everyone's okay, including you."

Janet was going to say something but held it back. She got into bed and pulled the sheet over herself.

"I had lunch with Dr. Holbrook. It's your turn to grab something, Jill."

A look of terror swept Janet's face, and she grabbed Jill's hand. "No!" she wailed.

I felt like an idiot for not appreciating the depth of Janet's trauma and the effect being trapped in a room alone with a strange man would cause. "I'll bring you a salad. Is Italian dressing okay?"

Jill comforted our patient and excused herself. She steered me into the hall. "I'm new to the protecting people stuff. Do I have my hand on my gun all the time? Should I sit in the hallway so I can see someone coming?"

I wrapped my arms around her. "No one knows she's here, so no one's coming. Just be vigilant and make sure Janet doesn't use the phone or get away."

"I saw how quickly you went for your gun in the ER."

"It was an over-reaction. Everything is under control. Get in there before Janet calls her friends to tell them about her exciting week."

Jill's eyes went wide. "Geez! I think I'll unplug the phone." She dashed into the room.

I was halfway down the hall when Jill called after me. "Our patient would like a can of Coke."

I waved acknowledgment and went to the elevator.

There was a half-full bowl of baby spinach and shredded carrots in my hand when I felt the phone vibrate in my pocket. "Fletcher," I said, balancing the bowl in one hand.

"Doug Fletcher?"

"Yes," I replied to the unfamiliar male voice.

"Ray West, from the Presidential Secret Service detail. I was told that you could update me on the status of the missing canoeists."

I looked at the caller ID that said the number was blocked. "Wrong number." I disconnected the call, assuming that some smart reporter had used social engineering to get someone to reveal my phone number. I was pouring dressing on Jill's salad when the phone vibrated again. This time I checked the caller ID, saw that the number was blocked and didn't answer. It rang a third time as I paid for the salad, Coke, and two bottles, of iced tea.

This time the caller ID shorthand suggested it was from the National Park Service. "Fletcher."

"Doug? This is Cheryl. Some guy from the Secret Service has been trying to call you. He said you hung up on him, then stopped answering your phone."

"Is he there with you?"

"No, he called my office, looking for an update. I thought it would be better coming from you."

"What did the caller ID say?"

"The number was blocked."

"It was probably a reporter, trying to get a scoop. Please don't give my number to anyone who's not showing you a badge."

"Really? I thought…"

"I'm serious." My thoughts ran away. "You didn't give him Jill's number, did you?"

"When you didn't answer…"

I stuffed the phone in my pocket and ran for the elevator.

Jill was on her cellphone when I ran into the room, startling her. I set the drinks and salad on the tray table.

"The Secret Service?" I asked.

Jill nodded, and I held out my hand. She passed her phone to me, and I verified that the caller ID was blocked. "Give me your number, and I'll call you right back."

"We don't give out our cellphone numbers…" I ended the call and handed the phone back to Jill.

"You hung up on the Secret Service?"

I handed her the salad. "It was a reporter who got your number from Cheryl. How much did you tell him?"

"I told him he needed to talk to you. He said your phone was off, and he needed the information urgently."

"What did you tell him?"

"Nothing. I said if you weren't available, he'd have to call the FBI."

"You were perfect."

I handed the Coke to Janet, who'd been listening in stunned silence. "What's going on?"

"People are trying to find you."

Jill glared at me while she opened the plastic clamshell with her salad.

"What?" I asked.

"You run in here like a raging bull and snatch the phone out of my hand."

I put up my hands. "I'm sorry. He'd almost got me, then I spoke with Cheryl, who'd given him our phone numbers."

Janet almost dropped her Coke. "You talked to Aunt Cheryl?"

"Briefly."

"Call her back."

A wave of understanding swept over Jill. "No, honey. We can't let anyone know. Not even Aunt Cheryl. If we'd told her you were safe, she would've told the reporter who was trying to get that information out of us."

My phone vibrated again, and I walked into the hallway. "Hi, Cheryl."

"You cut me off."

"Sorry. I had to get to Jill before she spoke to the reporter."

"What's the big secret. The media knows we found Dave's body yesterday."

"The FBI is in sensitive negotiations with the kidnappers. We don't want something to leak that would ruin the negotiations and interfere with Janet's release." The lie came much too quickly, but I reasoned it was necessary. Then I reflected on the number of times I'd been cut out of FBI cases. *But Cheryl is emotionally invested in the case, and sharing could easily lead to an unfortunate release of information.*

"Oh. Yeah. Good point. Where's the FBI at on the negotiations?"

"I heard they're close, but please don't share that with anyone."

"But if my brother calls…"

"He'll know what's going on, and no one else needs to know."

"You make it sound like a state secret."

"Cheryl, your niece's life may depend on your silence. We're at a point where anyone

205

who doesn't need to know information is kept in the dark."

"I think you're being overly dramatic."

"Trust me. I'm not dramatic. Things are extremely sensitive right now, and everything could go to hell. If the wrong tidbit of information leaked to the press, the kidnappers could be gone without releasing your niece."

Cheryl waited for a few beats. "Are you guys still checking the scout camps and the Catholic retreat?"

"We're done with that. Now we're checking with some of the residents along the river."

"Okay. Let me know if you hear anything."

I ended the call and punched in Maggie's number. "What?"

"We had someone claiming to be a Secret Service agent attempt to social engineer access to us through the park superintendent. They called from a blocked number, and we didn't provide anything to them."

"Shit."

"What's going on?"

"I can't comment right now."

"Maggie, we just got the victim moved to a remote part of the hospital where we're farther from prying eyes. We're your partners in this. What's going on?"

"Encrypted files were just transmitted to the IP address supplied by the kidnappers. They've received them and will have a fit any second when they realize they can't crack the encryption. It's going to generate a flurry of threats to kill the hostage and follow-up calls demanding the encryption key. I don't understand all the electronics and internet jargon, but there are smart people following the breadcrumbs."

"Are you closing in on their location?"

"They're not in the Twin Cities anymore. The last call came from Iowa."

"They never intended to release the hostage."

"I think we both knew that. We're fortunate we found her alive."

"*We* didn't find her alive. Jill and I found her alive with the help of a scout camp ranger. It'd be nice if that were clear when you have the news conference."

"I thought you were a team player who handed out accolades to everyone involved in your cases."

"I do. The FBI's involvement in recovering the man's body and rescuing the woman was nothing. Nada. It was the National Park Service, the Polk County sheriff's department, and a scout camp ranger."

Maggie let out a sigh. "Yes, you've done well. I've got to run. We've got feds and local cops scrambling over the Midwest, and I need to stay on top of that. Please keep the victim under wraps. I'll call when things get locked down."

"You'll call before the press conference."

"Of course."

I checked the hallway to ensure no one had been listening, walked back into the hospital room, and closed the door. Jill nibbled at the salad I'd brought, and Janet clutched her soda can like it might be taken away.

"Did you tell Aunt Cheryl I was okay? Is she calling my mom and dad?"

"Your dad is up to his eyeballs with the FBI right now. They're trying to locate the kidnappers electronically."

"But he knows I'm safe."

"Not yet. It's complicated, but the FBI expects the kidnappers to call back threatening to kill you, and they need him to sound like he believes they've still got you. The best way to ensure that he sounds scared is for him not to know you're safe."

"How can they threaten to kill me when I'm...Am I safe?"

"No one knows you're here, and you've got Jill and me with you. I promise we'd lay down our lives to keep you safe if needed."

Janet looked between us. "Shouldn't one of you be in the hall or something?"

"At this point, having me in the hall would only attract attention to this empty floor. Besides, the last call from the kidnappers came from Iowa."

"There must be one left behind who was going to release me."

I weighed my words. "They've fled the area. I think they were probably planning to tell your father where they'd stashed you once they had what they wanted."

Janet thought about that, then her eyes bored holes in me. "You're lying. I remember what that guy said to Jimbo. They weren't going to…"

The soda can fell out of Janet's hand and rolled across the bed before falling to the floor. Jill set her salad aside and took Janet in her arms. I picked up the can and wiped up spilled soda pop from the tile.

"See if there's a dry hospital gown in the closet."

I opened the cabinets and found a stack of gowns inside and handed one to Jill.

"Why don't you check with the nurse's station to get some dry sheets."

I shook my head. "I'll pull sheets off the bed next door. I don't want anyone down here who doesn't need to be here."

There was a knock on the door, and it started to open. I had the Sig out as I heard a female voice say, "Your lunch is here."

A smiling Hispanic woman stepped into the room with a food tray. The tray was covered with a plastic lid.

Jill stepped around the bed and reached out for the tray. The deliverywoman was unaware of me behind her with a gun in my hand.

"Jill, lift the cover."

When I spoke, the woman turned her head. Her eyes went wide when she saw the gun, then my uniform and badge. I made sure she wasn't reaching for a weapon, but the surprise on her face looked genuine.

"Sorry! I'm only bringing lunch." She held up her hands while Jill uncovered the tray with coffee, chicken broth, sorbet, and green Jell-O.

"We're okay," Jill said.

I lowered the gun. "I'm sorry. We didn't know you were coming."

The woman slowly lowered her hands. "It's okay?"

"Okay," I said, keeping the gun in my hand but next to my leg. "Who's the meal for?"

"What?" The woman asked, still rattled.

"Whose name is on the delivery?"

"No name. It says room two twelve."

I nodded and noted the woman's hospital ID that said her name was Miranda. We walked to the door and into the hallway. "I'm sorry I scared you. The woman is being protected. You can't tell anyone what happened."

"They don't know there are cops in her room?"

"No one should know there are cops in the room. You can't tell anyone. The woman's safety depends on people not knowing she's there. Okay?"

The woman studied my badge for a moment, then looked at me. "Okay."

I was sure everyone in food service would know about the cops protecting the woman in room two twelve as soon as Miranda got to the kitchen. I didn't know what else to do short of locking down the hospital door, and that would

210

bring more attention than gossiping kitchen employees.

I rapped on the door, and Jill told me to wait a moment.

"Okay. Come in."

Janet was in a dry hospital gown with the sodden one on the floor in the bathroom. Jill watched Janet eat as if she was starving, which was probably the case.

Another knock on the door spun me around, drawing the pistol as Dr. Holbrook's head peeked in. "How's the patient?"

I took a breath. "She's eating."

Holbrook nodded, took Janet's pulse, and gently pinched her skin. "Well, my dear, it appears that you're adequately hydrated. I'll have a nurse pull your IV lines. Please drink up all the fluids on your lunch tray and call the nurse if you'd like water, coffee, tea, or juice."

I shook my head, "Can you pull the IV line? I don't want any more people in here than necessary."

"I don't have any supplies. I'll get Belle up here to take care of it. Janet, would you like some juice?"

"Apple juice sounds really good."

The doctor nodded, and I followed her into the hallway. "Is she recovered?"

"Physically, yes. She's rehydrated, and the Benadryl we gave her seems to be reducing swelling from the bug bites. She's going to be messed up, suffering from PTSD. She'll undoubtedly have a meltdown when she finds out about her husband, and at some point, she's going to crash. She'll need some time with a good therapist to work through her trauma."

I put out my hand. "Thanks, doc."

Holbrook shook my hand. "Sorry, I was a little hard on you before. I'm unaccustomed to being ordered around."

My cellphone buzzed. "Fletcher."

"Doug, what's going on?"

"What do you mean, Cheryl?"

"I spoke with the search teams and the sheriff's department. They didn't find any sign of Janet, and no one's seen you or Jill."

"Something's come up, and we're busy. It looks like we'll be tied up for the rest of the day. Can I call you tomorrow?"

"What's up?"

"I can't say right now."

"You found Janet's body, and you're not telling me."

"I swear, Cheryl, Janet's alive as far as I know. The FBI is negotiating her release."

"You're not lying to protect me?"

"We're just waiting to hear from the FBI."

"You'll call as soon as you know something." She stated it as an order, not a question.

"Absolutely." Idisconnected the call before the conversation could continue, rechecked the empty hallway, and then went into Janet's room. She was teary, so I looked at Jill for a reason.

"Janet has a question I couldn't answer."

"What do you need?"

"You said I was kidnapped. Are the kidnappers asking for a ransom?"

"They contacted your father."

"What do they want?"

"Classified information from his company."

Janet's glance toward Jill made me uneasy. She'd drilled down to something Jill didn't want to address.

"Since you've rescued me, he's not giving it to them, right?"

"He's working with the FBI, and they're putting together something that looks convincing but isn't the classified files they want."

"And dad's negotiating for my release."

I suddenly realized Janet's destination. Once again, I'd been playing checkers against Janet, who was playing chess. "Yes."

"What ransom are they asking for Dave's release?" Her eyes bored into me, and there wasn't a convenient lie to her direct question.

I shook my head.

"I've been asking you the wrong question. You don't know where Dave is, but you know he's dead, right?"

I looked at Jill, who raised her eyebrows, hinting it was time to fess up. "Yes."

Janet's chin fell, and her chest heaved as she sobbed.

Jill jumped up and handed her a tissue.

Janet's breathing became even, and she drew a deep breath before looking at me again. "You could've told me right away?"

"You were a mess and needed to worry about your own health. There was nothing any of us could do about Dave."

"The kidnappers didn't need him."

"You were leverage for the kidnappers to get to your father. Dave was irrelevant to them. They needed you to talk to your father at least once to prove you were alive." I sat on the edge of the bed and attempted to grasp her hand in empathy, but she pulled away from me. My phone buzzed, and I got up to answer it in the hall. The caller ID showed Maggie Steller's number. "Fletcher."

"Ask our patient if the guys who kidnapped her had Chicago accents."

I walked back into the room. "Why? What's up?"

"Ask."

"I'll hand her the phone."

Janet took the phone. "Who is this?" She listened carefully, saying, "uh, huh," a couple of times. Then she asked to speak with her father. Maggie apparently handed the phone to him because there were sobbing and questions.

I made a phone sign to Jill and mouthed, *call Cheryl.* Jill took out her cellphone and walked to the hallway.

Janet wiped her tears on the back of her hand and sniffled. "Yeah, he's still here." I reached for the phone, but the conversation continued. Janet stared at me as Maggie said something I couldn't hear. Then she handed me the phone.

"Maggie, is it over?"

"Our part is. The U.S. Marshals from Des Moines and FBI agents from Sioux Falls are closing in on a truck with two men who've been on the phone with us. Whatever happens from here is out of my hands."

"What should we do with Janet?"

"A state trooper is bringing her mother to the hospital. They're probably forty-five minutes away. We'll bring her father over after we finish debriefing him."

"I imagine he reamed you thoroughly for keeping Janet's situation from him."

"I've got pretty thick skin, Fletcher, and more skilled people than him have reamed me."

"Tell him Janet's doing very well. She's sitting up and has eaten solid food."

"I'll pass that along." Maggie paused. "Does Janet know about her husband?"

"We were just having that discussion when you called."

"Fletcher…"

"You've got something else?"

"You and Jill were great. If you hadn't burned every bridge with the FBI in the past, I'd suggest that you apply to be special agents."

I laughed. "Yeah, that's off the table."

"In all seriousness, you and Jill saved that girl. I told both Janet and her father that, but you should hear it from someone farther up the chain of command in the next day or two."

"I don't imagine it'll make up for all the 'aw shits.'"

Maggie laughed. "Oh, I'm sure it won't. The bureau has a long memory."

I ended the call with Janet staring at me. "Was she really an FBI special agent."

"Yes. She was coordinating your kidnapping investigation. She's the one who asked us to keep you out of the public eye while they negotiated with the kidnappers."

"She asked you, not ordered you."

"Jill and I understood the situation. We didn't need to be 'ordered' to protect you and your security. It was our duty."

"She told me to thank you. If you two hadn't found me, I would still be lying in that old cabin being eaten by mosquitoes."

"I don't know what would've happened. The National Park Service and sheriff's departments all had people out searching. I think someone would've found you."

I had a brief flash and turned to Janet. "Do you have any idea how the kidnappers knew you'd be on the river?"

Janet looked at the floor. "I put it on Facebook. I suppose someone looked at my homepage."

"You put it on Facebook?"

Janet shrugged. "My friends and I are always posting pictures of the places we're at and the plans we're making."

Jill walked in, smiling. "Aunt Cheryl's on her way."

Janet nodded and wiggled her fingers for Jill to come closer. Janet put out her hand, then pulled Jill into a hug that almost pulled her off her feet. I got pulled into a hug next.

Janet wiped tears from her eyes with the back of her hand. "You two are partners?"

Jill nodded. "In work and life. We're married."

That revelation left Janet silent. "I'm probably the age of your kids."

Jill shook her head. "No kids. I've been married to my career too long."

I redirected the conversation. "Hey! I'm going to see if the nurse's station has some scrubs you can wear so we can get you out of that hospital gown."

* * *

I returned, carrying a pile of clothing, to an earnest discussion. "They have scrubs for the operating room but no underwear. But one of the nurses found a box of Depends they give to their incontinent patients."

Janet raised her eyebrows. "Now I know you're joking."

I held up the plastic wrapper. "No joke."

Janet shook her head. "I suppose it's better than going commando in a pair of starched scrubs."

I handed her the clothing and stepped into the hall. Jill followed a minute later and leaned against me. "Can we go back to the Inn when Cheryl gets here?"

"I think we have to make a handoff to the FBI before we can go."

"I could really use a hot bath and a glass of wine."

Chapter Fourteen

The rest of the afternoon was a blur. Cheryl swept in like a tornado and alternated between hugging Janet and berating me for not telling her Janet was safe. Jill, not being part of those discussions, was an angel and given credit for rescuing Janet while I stood in the corner.

Janet's mother, Shelly, walked in ahead of a stern-looking Minnesota State Trooper. She and Cheryl were in tears. We "cops" were superfluous to their celebration, so we walked into the hall. The trooper, seeing that things were under control, excused himself.

Jill leaned on my arm. "At some point, they're going to crash and have to deal with the loss of Dave." Jill pushed me back and looked stricken. "Do we have to notify his family?"

I pulled her back. "The sheriff's department has already taken care of that."

"We got the happy end of this...this mess."

"Definitely."

"Are you rebooking us for flights tomorrow?"

"We're not done here."

"What?"

"The President's kid is coming, and we don't know who posted the video of the nude rangers on the internet."

"Just when I was starting to let the adrenaline seep out of my system."

Two men in suits appeared out of the elevator. One's suit was rumpled like he hadn't changed it in two days, and the other's was as crisp as if he'd just taken it out of the dry cleaner's bag. I waved to them.

"Who are they?"

"I'm sure the one who looks like he's been dragged behind a horse is Janet's father. The other looks like he's wearing the FBI uniform."

I opened the door. "Janet's in here."

The rumpled man's face looked gray and haggard. He stopped in front of me for a second and glanced at my uniform. "I heard a National Park Service ranger found my daughter. Was that you?"

I nodded toward Jill. "My partner and I were searching with a ranger at the scout camp."

"Bill Elliot," he said, reaching out his hand. "I can't thank you enough."

Jill hung back, but I pulled her forward. "This is my partner, Jill Fletcher."

Elliot shook her hand with his eyes glistening. He went into the hospital room, and the FBI agent introduced himself as Ron Norris. "The Special Agent in Charge (SAC) would like you two to come to the Minneapolis office tomorrow at nine forty-five."

"We're expected at the park tomorrow for a briefing before the President's son arrives."

Norris shook his head. "Call your boss. I'm sure that has changed." He looked at our uniforms, dirty from crawling through the underbrush, and rumpled from sitting in them all day at the hospital. "You should freshen up your uniforms for the press conference."

I tilted my head back. "I don't think…"

Norris shook his head. "Think of it as an order, not an offer or request."

I was tired and irritable, ready to release a profane tirade. Jill grabbed my arm as I stated, "We're turning our victim over to you, Special Agent Norris. We were in the woods all morning and require our motel room to do a tick inspection."

Norris nodded. "Good idea. Find the ticks before they attach."

* * *

"Are you serious about tick inspection?" Jill smiled as I drove through downtown Stillwater to our Inn. "Or was it an excuse for a quick exit."

I raised my eyebrows. "I thought it could be interesting."

* * *

Jill beat me into the bathroom and locked the door.

"I thought we were going to inspect each other for ticks."

"I've got it covered. See if you can get a table at the wine bar while I shower."

I called the front desk, thinking they might have more leverage with the restaurant than I would. The front desk called back five minutes later, saying he'd reserved the last available table, and we had to be there in twenty minutes.

I knocked on the bathroom door while the shower still pounded inside. "Reservation in twenty minutes."

The shower stopped. "What?"

"We have a reservation for the last table open tonight in twenty minutes."

"My hair won't be dry in twenty minutes!"

"Hey, I only did what you requested."

The bathroom lock clicked. "You'd better hop in the shower while I dry off."

I stripped off my uniform and laid it on the bed, then walked into the bathroom naked. Jill had a towel wrapped around her torso and used another to dry her hair. I tugged at the edge of the wrapped towel, and it slipped free.

"Let's skip the restaurant."

Jill caught the towel before it came loose. "You smell like a sweaty swamp. Take a shower and get dressed. I need to unwind, not get revved up." She was out of the bathroom before I could respond.

* * *

The wine bar was busy and noisy. The owner recognized us, meeting us at the door. "I'm full tonight. A couple of bar stools look like they're about ready to open up if you want to wait here."

"The Inn called and said you had a table for two."

"Of course! I didn't connect you two with Angie's call. You've got the table in the back corner, past the end of the bar."

He led us to the table, and I took the chair facing the door. He handed us menus and took Jill's order for a glass of a New Zealand red wine. I ordered tonic and lime. The metal ceiling made the room noisy.

I leaned across the table. "We could try someplace quieter."

Jill shook her head. "This is perfect. I want to be around people. I want to feel alive."

The women next to us were well into their wine and passing presents to a woman celebrating her birthday. The more they drank, the louder they got.

"But we can't talk."

Jill reached out and took my hand. She squeezed it and smiled. "This is what I need tonight."

* * *

The owner came over to our table as the crowd thinned. "I apologize for putting you next to the birthday crew. I don't imagine you got a chance to say anything with their celebration so close. Can I buy you dessert?"

I put my hand up. "You're too late. I've been overserved."

Jill smiled. "If I could have a scoop of vanilla ice cream, I'd be in hog heaven."

He was back in five minutes with Jill's ice cream topped with a drizzle of Port wine. After putting it in front of Jill, he pulled a chair from a nearby table and sat down. "The Inn said you're honeymooners."

Jill dabbled at her ice cream, making yummy noises, so I guessed responding was my responsibility. "We didn't have time for a honeymoon when we got married last year, so we're doing it now."

"The Inn also said you're Texas cops."

"We're National Park Service investigators from Texas."

"And you chose Stillwater for your honeymoon?"

"We're helping search for the couple who disappeared from the river last week."

"Are you having any luck?"

I nodded. "We've made some progress."

He gave me a cagey smile. "You're not saying anymore, are you?"

"Not tonight."

He got up and patted my shoulder. "You're a lucky man to be married to this classy woman."

Jill had a silly grin, and I wasn't sure if it was because of the compliment or the wine. She pushed the remaining half-scoop of ice cream to me and wiped her lips. "He was very kind, but I still think I got the better end of the marriage deal."

I ate one spoonful of the ice cream while I tried to find the right words. "You complete me." I signaled the owner for the bill.

He shook his head and pointed his hand toward the door and bowed from the far end of the restaurant.

"Do you have any cash?" I asked.

"I've probably got twenty or thirty bucks. Why don't you pay with a card?"

"He's refusing to bring us a check, and I want to leave a generous tip for the busboy and chef."

We walked to the end of the bar, and I palmed forty dollars that I put into the owner's hand when we shook. He tried to give it back. "It's a tip. Okay?"

He nodded and held the door for us as we stepped out. "Will you be back tomorrow night?"

"I'm not sure where we'll be or what time we'll eat tomorrow."

"It'll be slower. There'll be a table for you whenever you get free."

Jill leaned against me. "Thank you. We had a lovely dinner."

"Ma'am, you raised the class in this place by fifty percent. I love having polite, friendly folks like you in house. You make the place feel classy."

Jill hung on my arm as we walked down the sidewalk toward the Inn. "Imagine that, a South Dakota ranch girl and a St. Paul cop making a nice wine bar into a classier place."

I kissed the top of her head. "You make every place classier."

Jill put on her best Mandy Mattson southern drawl. "Inspector Fletcher, I do believe you just charmed my pants off."

We walked in silence, arm in arm. "I get the feeling you're making up for fifty years of self-imposed celibacy."

Jill squeezed my arm. "What's the matter? Do you think I only want you for your body?"

"I just...I've never met a woman who was as interested in the bedroom as you are."

"Maybe, I'm using your love to escape some of the horrors of the world." She paused. "Or maybe you've shown me that making love is more than doing my wifely duty."

"Huh?"

"You said something about ranch kids knowing about sex through animal husbandry. I saw the mechanics of sex, but the bull enjoys it a lot more than the cow. It's even starker with horses where the mare is sometimes injured. When Mom and I had 'the talk,' she explained a woman's role as pleasing her husband. You...make sure I enjoy the experience as much as you."

"That's what love is."

226

"Not that I have a lot of experience, but it seems like there are a lot of men who are into 'wham, bam, thank you, ma'am.'"

I digested that on the rest of the stroll back to the Inn. We walked into the lobby and were met by the desk clerk who waved. "I've got a couple messages for you."

I patted my pocket and realized I'd left my cellphone in the dirty uniform pants in my rush to shower and dress for dinner. I took three message slips and thanked the clerk. Jill read over my shoulder as we waited for the elevator.

"It looks like Matt isn't pleased that your phone is off again."

"Yeah. I'm sure he's just making sure we're going to the news conference. I'm more intrigued by the messages from Jess Pond and Maggie Steller. They only left call back numbers."

Jill took the messages out of my hand and folded them. "They'll wait until morning."

I touched her face. "You said that like you actually believed it."

"Priorities, dear."

I unlocked the bedroom and snatched the slips out of her hand. "You go freshen up and put on something that'll distract me."

Jill looked unhappy but pulled something out of her suitcase and went into the bathroom. I prioritized the messages, deciding Matt was looking for an update, Jess had something about our internet search that wasn't urgent, and

Maggie might have something that could change our morning plans.

I heard the shower start as I punched in Maggie's number. "Hi, Maggie. You left a message."

"Do you turn off your phone every evening?"

"It fell out of my pocket while I was changing for dinner."

"The U.S. Marshals caught up with the guys making the kidnapping demands before they hit the South Dakota border. They'd downloaded the files, uploading them to a remote server, using 4G that faded in and out. They dismantled their phones and computer, throwing the pieces onto the highway before they got boxed in and stopped. They shouted that they wanted lawyers before getting out of their vehicle."

"So, you don't know who they were selling to?"

"I didn't say that. We'd intercepted all their activity for most of the day, getting their data transmissions and phone conversations live. The local cops and state patrol recovered most of the electronics from the road, but they're only icing on the cake if we recover anything from them."

"I don't suppose they offered the location of the kidnap victim?"

"Their lawyer offered that in return for a plea deal. He was incredibly surprised that we didn't care, so he and his clients are huddled together, figuring out what to do next."

I heard the shower stop. "Anything else?"

"You and Jill were key to pulling this off. Because we have Janet Eastman, those clowns are either going to jail for a long, long time or will have to come up with something spectacular to get a shorter sentence. Either way, they're going to prison."

"Thanks."

"You and Jill are still expected to be at the news conference. I heard you like to slip out of them, and that's not an option. Understood?"

Jill walked out of the bathroom in a short nightie that wasn't revealing but was a huge step away from an ankle-length flannel nightgown. "We'll be there. I've got to run."

"Your National Park Service boss asked me to have you call if I heard from you."

I ended the call without answering her.

Jill walked over and sat on my lap, taking the phone from my hand, throwing it onto a chair, and putting her arm around my shoulders.

"That was Maggie…"

Jill put her finger to my lips. "I don't want to hear about it tonight."

"They…"

She nuzzled my neck. "Shh."

* * *

Morning seemed to come especially early. I'd opened the window, and the birds were chirping at five o'clock. I slipped out of bed, picked up Jill's nightie and my clothes from the floor, showered, and pinned the National Park Service insignias and badges on our fresh uniforms.

Jill rolled over, pulled the sheet up to her neck, and watched.

"You don't have to pull the sheet to your neck like a spinster."

She smiled, displaying her dazzling dimples. "I'm trying to maintain the mystery."

"I think that mystery has been solved."

"I want it to be like the movie *Groundhog Day*, where we rediscover it daily."

I took a bulky robe from the back of the bathroom door and handed it to her. "I'll return more calls while you're in the shower."

Jill pulled the robe around her shoulders and somehow got out of bed without flashing any more skin than I'd seen in a Doris Day movie. I picked up the phone and scrolled through messages. Since we were an hour later than South Dakota, I decided to call Matt before calling Jess Pond in the mountain time zone.

"Doug! You've got to stop turning off your phone. I had calls all night from people trying to reach you. Somehow, they thought I could transport myself to Minnesota and get you out of bed. By the way, the switchboard at the Inn cuts off all calls at ten o'clock."

"Perfect!"

"It's not perfect! I did everything short of having Cheryl Britton go over and knock down your door."

"That might've been embarrassing."

Matt sighed. "There isn't anything I can say to rattle you, is there?"

"Not unless you're telling me there's an incoming nuclear missile."

"You are going to the FBI news conference."

"Is that a question?"

"Hell, no! That's an order from my boss's boss. You will be there. Do I need to send a National Park Service escort to make sure you make it on time?"

"I was just pinning the insignias on fresh uniforms."

"I suppose it's too much to hope that you have dress uniforms there."

"Yes, that's too much to hope for. Just be happy that we have clean uniforms. The ones we wore yesterday are pretty dirty and gamy."

Matt's voice softened. "Maggie Steller and Cheryl Britten both called to update me on what you and Jill did yesterday. I can't imagine the relief Cheryl's family had once they heard you had their daughter safely hidden away. That's pretty spectacular."

"Thanks. Anything else?"

"I'm sure this will be a letdown, but you and Jill are still needed for assistance with security during the President's son's visit."

"I'd guessed that. We're also still tracking down the source of the internet posts that are causing Cheryl's headaches."

"I'd forgotten about her Human Resources problem. Are you making any headway?"

"I was just going to call my FBI contact who's got his computer experts working on it."

Jill walked out of the bathroom in her sports bra and granny panties. "Are you talking to Matt?"

I handed the phone to her. "Hey, Matt. How's life in Texas?" She carried the phone into the bathroom and closed the door. Whatever topic she discussed was apparently a secret.

I laid out Jill's uniform and got our Smokey Bear hats out of the closet. Jill returned and handed me the phone.

"What's the secret?"

She looked surprised by the question.

"You took my phone and locked yourself in the bathroom. Something's going on you obviously didn't want me to hear."

"Mandy and the girls are planning something. I didn't want to bore you with girl stuff. Have you called Jess Pond yet?"

I entered Jess' cellphone number. "Hi, Jess. You left a message last night."

"I've got to get a National Park Service job where I can work 9 to 5 and turn off my phone at the end of my shift. Do you get weekends off too?"

"Jess, you're overqualified and too intense for the National Park Service."

"I've got some information about your internet posts. The good news is we got the internet address of the person who uploaded the video. The bad news is, we may not know who the person actually is, and the location is going to be challenging."

Jill took the phone from me and turned on the speaker feature. "We don't understand what you're saying."

"The account who uploaded the videos is a Gmail ID. Anyone can get one using any screen name they choose. Sometimes that's irrelevant if the person logged in from home or a fixed IP location. Whoever this is has been logging on using libraries and coffee shop Wi-Fi over a lot of northwestern Wisconsin."

Jill leaned close to the phone. "So, he's probably using a fake name, is moving around, and is on untraceable Wi-Fi."

"That's pretty much it exactly. The video was uploaded from a coffee shop in Marine-on-the St. Croix. We checked with the owner, and he doesn't have a camera, plus they're on a bike trail and have hundreds of people who log onto the Wi-Fi a day. It's a dead end."

"Is there any good news?" I asked.

"There is. He logs onto the Wi-Fi at the Osceola, Wisconsin library every other day to check his email. He always logs on early in the morning or in the evening, which makes me think he has a daytime job. We also have a list of his email contacts, and some of them have fixed IP locations and real names."

"Can you lean on them and find out who it is?"

"I've got an agent trying to associate the email addresses with physical addresses and phone numbers. I don't hold out much hope for being able to call these people. There are too many scammers making calls and identifying themselves as IRS or other feds, but we may be able to get someone to knock on a couple doors."

"Excellent!"

"Hey, we're not picking up the whole load here. I've got one for you." Jess read a cryptic email name to me and gave me an address in Somerset, Wisconsin. "It's an apartment building."

"We'll check it out later today."

Chapter Fifteen

Jill seemed at ease driving through the countryside and St. Paul's eastern suburbs. The speed limit dropped to 55, and we slowed as we went under the 694/494 loop. We passed a small lake, a campus of poured concrete, and brick buildings. A red 3M logo topped the tallest building.

"Is this where they make Post-it notes?"

"These buildings are the headquarters and research labs. I don't think they make anything here."

From there, I-94 twisted along a bend in the Mississippi River. Just before downtown, there was a tall building with SPPD on top. "Is that where you worked?"

"I spent most of my career working out of a precinct building or the old headquarters, downtown."

"Where does your mom live?"

"She's north of here, in Roseville. We can take highway 36 back, and we'll go within a couple miles of her house."

Traffic slowed further as we got close to the University of Minnesota. "I lived a couple blocks from here when I was married. Sherry wanted to be close to the school."

"You haven't mentioned her. Ronnie told me she was a pretty, smart leech, who sucked you dry financially and emotionally."

I patted Jill's hand. "I don't want to dwell on what was. I'm in a much better place now."

Downtown Minneapolis was like any other major metropolis, jammed with traffic and people. I pointed toward a parking ramp a few blocks from the federal courthouse. Jill parked, and then we walked, wearing our Smokey Bear hats, and garnering a few glances.

I stopped in front of the federal courthouse and dialed Maggie's cellphone.

"Jill and I are on the sidewalk out front. Where do you want us?"

"Huh. You showed up. Odds were running 3:1 against, but I was betting on you." She paused. "The news conference will be in a third-floor conference room. Take the elevator after you go through security."

Maggie waited for us outside the conference room, dressed in a nicely tailored, dark pin-striped suit with an ivory blouse. Her eyes were glued to her cellphone screen. She looked up when she sensed our presence.

"I love the hats," she said, closing her phone. She led us into the conference room to empty chairs behind a dais with a dozen microphones mounted on it. She checked her watch. "There's probably not time for a cup of coffee, but I can show you where the bathrooms are."

Jill and Maggie left through a side door. I checked messages and was surprised when a pair of hunting boots showed up in my downward vision. I looked up at Chris Locker's nervous face. He wore a scout leader's uniform, and I recognized the "knots" over his left pocket for Scouting's highest awards, the Eagle, and Silver Beaver.

He looked around nervously. "I don't want to be here, but Karen said I had to come when she heard I'd been invited."

"If it's any consolation, I don't want to be here either, but here we are, resplendent in our uniforms."

Jill and Maggie returned. Neither seemed surprised to see Chris. Maggie shook his hand. "I'm glad you changed your mind."

"You pulled a fast one on me by telling my wife."

Maggie smiled. "I am devious when I need to be."

The chatter ended when a man carrying a portfolio walked into the room and stepped to the dais. I was ready to sit when I felt Maggie's hand on my elbow. She kept Jill, Chris, and me standing.

"Ladies and gentlemen. I believe each of you has a copy of my prepared comments. There will be an opportunity for questions at the conclusion of my remarks." The speaker, who I recognized as the SAC of the Minneapolis FBI office, paused as he opened his portfolio and stared at his notes.

"Yesterday afternoon, we arrested two men in connection with the kidnapping of a young couple who were canoeing on the St. Croix River. With the assistance of members from the U.S. National Park Service and the scout camp ranger, we rescued the kidnap victim prior to the capture of the kidnappers. I want to thank Jill Fletcher, Doug Fletcher, and Chris Locker for their heroic actions. Because of them, the female victim is alive and with her family."

The conference went on for another five minutes, but I didn't hear any of it. I watched reporters jockeying for position, trying to be recognized, so they could ask their repetitive questions for their stations and networks to get a sound bite for *their* news broadcast.

I caught my name being thrown out but missed the question. Maggie looked at me expectantly, like I should step forward and answer. I put my hand on Jill's back and pushed her toward the podium. She was too polished and professional to give me the glare I'm sure she wanted to share.

"Inspector Doug Fletcher and I are married. We were assigned to the investigation by our Texas superintendent because of our experience canoeing." The questions rang out, but Jill put up her hand. "Please let me say that without Chris Locker, the ranger at the Wisconsin scout camp, we never would've found the victim, and she most likely would've died before anyone else found her. Please give him a hand."

There was a round of polite applause before the SAC regained control. I looked at Chris, who was blushing. "I wish she wouldn't have done that."

I shrugged and whispered out of the corner of my mouth. "She does what she does. I don't control her."

Jill stepped between Maggie and me. She smiled as she leaned close. "I'd kill you right now if all these people weren't watching."

"Your mom and dad will be delighted to see you on the network news."

The conference ended, and we were engulfed by reporters, who cut Chris and Jill away from me, grilling each of us with questions. After about fifteen minutes, Maggie rescued us shortly before the FBI cleared the room and the cameras shut down.

Jill was stalking me, and I pushed Chris between us. "Watch out for her elbows. They're deadly."

Maggie defused Jill's anger by hugging her. "You were fabulous, and you're much more photogenic than Doug."

Jill continued to glare at me but relaxed. "Thank you."

Chris looked like a deer in the headlights until Karen came through the crowd to hug him. I put out my hand. "I'm not sure if the scouts still give out a lifesaving award, but I'm going to call and recommend you for one."

Chris' armpits were dark with sweat, and he looked drained. "I think they only give that to scouts who make water rescues."

"We'll see."

Maggie sent Chris and Karen off and steered Jill and me to a corner. "I need your statements about the rescue and what Janet Eastman told you when she became lucid."

Jill took a deep breath. "The rape kit?"

"It's being processed. It takes a while for the DNA comparison."

"But there was DNA to test."

Maggie nodded.

Jill crossed her arms and stared into a corner while she processed the information.

* * *

Jill was silent as I drove out of Minneapolis. I knew she needed to talk, but I didn't want to intrude on her thoughts.

"The big shopping center on the left was the center of my teen life."

"Does Ronnie live near here?"

"North and about three blocks east."

"Drive me past the house where you grew up."

We wound through the old neighborhood, full of two-story houses on small lots. Each had slightly different architecture, but they'd all been built during the housing boom of the late '40s.

"Ours is the green one on the left. Do you want to stop?"

Jill shook her head. "No. Mom taught me never to drop in on anyone unannounced."

I went back to highway 36 and drove to Wisconsin. It was nearly mid-afternoon by the time we got to the National Park Service headquarters.

The headquarters parking lot was unusually busy, with more than half a dozen big SUVs and antennae bristling from their roofs. I found a spot near the back of the lot.

"It appears the Secret Service has arrived," I commented as we walked across the lot.

Jill looked awed by the aggregation of government vehicles. "How many Secret Service agents does it take to protect a teenager?"

"That's the opening to a joke. One to throw his body on the kid and six to point their guns at the crowd."

Jill hadn't forgiven me for pushing her to the microphones, so I got a withering glare as we opened the door.

I hadn't realized how steamy the parking lot was until the cool lobby air hit me in the face. More than a dozen people stood at the far end of the lobby with uniforms representing at least five police agencies. A man in a dark suit had his back to us and spoke to the crowd.

Cheryl stood off to one side and waved us over. "The Secret Service is briefing us on the plans for tomorrow."

We nodded and caught the last few minutes of his statement. "Are there any questions?"

Heads were shaking, but the Polk County sheriff spoke up, "So, you're calling the shots, and all of us are marching to your tune?"

The stern male speaker, graying at the temples and wearing a neatly pressed suit, nodded his head. "You all have your assignments. If you're part of the group paddling the river, we'll have another briefing in the morning with specific canoe assignments."

The sheriff didn't look pleased but didn't press the issue.

I looked at Cheryl. "What did we miss?"

"You two are in canoes tomorrow."

Jill looked surprised. "Us?"

"You're armed representatives of the National Park Service. Bring your sunscreen and insect repellent. Most of the feds aren't smart enough to know about those precautions, so they're going to be sun-burned and eaten alive."

"You're not warning them?" Jill whispered.

"They've made it clear I can't tell them anything, so fuck 'em."

Jill smirked, surprised by Cheryl's profanity. "They've pissed you off?"

"They've taken over my park."

The man in the dark suit looked over the crowd once more. "Okay, if there aren't any more questions, I'll see your people in the morning."

The crowd dispersed. Some of the local sheriffs stepped aside to commiserate about being ordered around by the feds. The man in charge walked over to us and put out his hand without introducing himself. "I assume you're the National Park Service inspectors."

I shook his hand. "Doug and Jill Fletcher."

He sized us up, then looked at Cheryl. "I'm glad you found some rangers who look like they've graduated from high school."

Cheryl bristled at his comment but bit her tongue. "Doug and Jill are seasoned and are the best people you could ask for."

To change the topic, I spoke up, "What do you need from us?"

"Cheryl wants you in the flotilla with my agents. If anything comes up, our focus will be on the President's son. I want you to take responsibility for the safety of the rest of his classmates."

I seized up. *Holy shit! He thinks we're going to take over if something goes south, and he makes a run for safety with the kid.*

Jill was calm and collected. "We've got it."

The SAC bid us farewell. "I'll see you in the morning."

We watched him walk out, then I asked Cheryl, "Where have they got the kid stashed for the night?"

"I don't know specific details. They've taken over a campground, maybe in Willow River State Park, and I'm sure the place looks like an armed compound."

"It's not our problem," Jill said.

Cheryl nodded, then pointed to her office. She closed the door after we entered, then hugged Jill. Tears she'd been holding back during the briefing let loose in a torrent. "I prayed every day that someone would find Janet. I'd given up hope of her being alive." She let go of Jill and pulled me close, letting her tears fall on my shoulder.

I patted her back. Jill had tears in her eyes too. "I'm happy it turned out okay. Is Janet back with her parents?"

"Yes. She's got appointments with her gynecologist and a psychiatrist this morning, and then she's meeting Dave's parents at a funeral home this afternoon."

"Sounds like a scene from purgatory in Dante's Inferno," Jill said.

Cheryl pulled a box from her drawer and handed tissues to each of us. "I hope she's strong enough to get through this."

Jill wiped her eyes and blew her nose. "We all have reserves we can dip into during emergencies."

"Like when you pulled that deputy off the highway in Wyoming?" Cheryl asked.

Jill nodded. "Both physical and emotional strength come through when you need them."

Cheryl sat in her chair. "Tell me about finding Janet."

I shook my head and reached for a lie. She didn't need or want to know the details. "It's an ongoing investigation, and the FBI wants to keep the details under wraps until the trials."

Cheryl accepted my lie. "Over a beer someday."

Jill nodded. "We have some information about your HR issue."

"What do you know?"

Jill explained what we'd heard from the Rapid City FBI. "Whoever posted the video has been logging onto the internet from libraries over here. Somerset and Osceola are his usual haunts, and we've got an address in a Somerset apartment complex that we're going to check out."

Cheryl was ready to jump up. "Let's go!"

I put up my hand. "Let Jill and me handle it."

"But..."

"We're better prepared to deal with the situation if things get ugly."

Cheryl acquiesced. "What can I do?"

"Can you give us pictures of all your male rangers?"

Cheryl thought for a moment. "They're all in a file for creating IDs. Give me a minute to pull it up, and I'll print them for you."

"Print pictures of all your rangers, male and female," I said.

"The women too?"

"If we're showing them to librarians and the apartment manager, I'd like to have everyone. I don't want to look like we've biased our suspect pool."

Cheryl logged onto her computer while Jill and I stepped out of her office. "Why did you ask for the women too?" Jill asked.

"Our suspect is probably a man, but why narrow the field?"

Jill digested that and closed her eyes. "Some of my biggest problems were between the female rangers. I had to step into some real catfights."

"It's best to keep an open mind until the evidence points you to someone."

We used the bathrooms, found coffee, and went back to Cheryl's office just as the last photos printed out. "I don't have any photo paper, but the faces are recognizable. I'm afraid most of them look like driver's license pictures, but they're all I've got."

Cheryl had grouped the photos six to a page, mixing the hair colors and sexes somewhat randomly. I leafed through the pages quickly. "How did you pick the order of the pictures?"

"They're by date of hire. The top page people have been with the National Park Service the longest and are my permanent employees. Farther down are the seasonal hires who've been with me the shortest time."

"Perfect," I handed them back to Cheryl. "Make a copy of them."

Cheryl left for the copy machine.

"Why do we need two sets?"

"He's been using two libraries. I thought we'd split up and see if he logs in one place or the other."

"I'm not particularly comfortable confronting a pervert without backup."

"You don't have to confront him. All we have to do is identify him and let the local sheriff's department deal with him."

"But it's a National Park Service problem. Why involve the sheriff?"

"He's been doing this from outside the park. It's a local issue. After the arrest, we can involve the National Park Service HR to have him fired."

Cheryl had guessed my plan and handed a stack of photos to each of us. "Are you going to get into this after the Secret Service is gone?"

I got up. "We've got nothing else going on this afternoon. Can you give one of us a ride to Somerset or Osceola?"

Cheryl took a keyring out of her desk. "I've got a spare SUV this afternoon. You can drive yourself."

Chapter Sixteen

Jill went to Osceola, and I drove to the Somerset library. Two blocks away around the corner from the library, I found a parking spot out of sight from the building. As I walked down the sidewalk, it occurred that it was impossible to be incognito in my uniform. Even if I took my badge and shirt off, that still left me in the distinctive green National Park Service pants. My friend, Jamie, in the Navajo Nation Police laughingly described the color of my uniform pants as *calf shit green*. Jill disagreed with him, asserting that South Dakota calf shit was yellow. Being a city kid, I had no opinion.

A row of computers was in use beyond the librarian's desk, and I scanned the user's faces. Two were schoolchildren, and one was a senior citizen, so not my suspects. An older woman scanned books over an electronic reader behind the desk.

"Excuse me."

She looked up and smiled. "How can I help you?"

I spread my sheets of pictures on the counter. "Do you recognize any of these people?"

She quickly scanned the photos. "I don't, but I only volunteer here two afternoons a week. The director is in her office. She'd be a better resource for you."

The director sat at a computer looking at email. Her desk was covered with books and paper, leaving only her guest chair uncluttered. I cleared my throat, and she nearly flew out of the chair.

She glanced at my uniform. "Oh! Sorry. I didn't expect anyone."

I introduced myself and handed the sheets to her. "Please look at these photos. We're hoping to find someone who's been logging onto the internet from your computers."

I noticed *Shelby Long* embossed across a brass nameplate on her desk. She looked through the pictures quickly. "I don't recognize anyone. But I'm in my office a lot, and people come and go without me seeing their faces."

"Libraries have changed."

The young director pulled a stray hair behind her ear. "I'm sure you grew up with card catalogs and the Dewey Decimal System. We used to look things up in reference books for people. Now we're computer resources, and we do internet searches and show people how to use the computers for email. More than half our library is online."

"When are the other librarians around, Ms. Long?"

She stood up, read my nametag, and put out her hand. "I'm Shelby, Ranger Fletcher."

249

"Please call me Doug."

"Well, Doug, there's something else that's changed. My staff is nearly all volunteers, and they rotate days and shifts. A big chunk of my job is coordinating workers, so there's somebody behind the desk all the time."

"So, it might take a week for me to speak with all the people who cover your desk and see the computers."

"At least a week," Shelby said with a laugh. Her eyes brightened. "But we have a sign-in log for computer use. You can look through it to see if any of those people have logged onto the computer."

Shelby led me to a three-ring binder on a counter near the computer terminals. It read in bold letters that all users had to sign in and were limited to 30 minutes of use if people were waiting. The lines were filled with scrawled signatures and the printed names of younger children.

"Is there somewhere I can sit down and read through the pages?"

"There's a table near the window with a newspaper spread out. Have fun."

I flipped through the pages quickly, then had a brainstorm. I called Jess Pond.

"Jess, I'd like to know exactly which day and time our suspect was logged on in Somerset."

"You know, Fletcher, I'm not sitting here with information for you, just awaiting your next call."

"I know, but you seem to have the information when I need it."

Jess sighed, and I heard computer keys clicking. "Okay, he was online in Somerset at 4:45 last Thursday and at 5:10 Monday. Is that enough?"

"Yes. I'm looking at the computer sign-in logs at the library." I flipped back to the days and times but didn't see anyone signed in whose name was on my sheets. "I've got nothing. Jill's in Osceola. Give me the sign-on dates and times there too."

I wrote down the information and thanked him, then called Jill and told her what I was doing. Shelby was at her desk with her back to the door, so I cleared my throat again.

She spun around. "Did that work for you?"

"Our suspect wasn't in the logs. Are people religious about signing in?"

"I'd say most are good about it, and if it's busy, everyone signs in, or they get booted off when someone comes in who does sign in."

"Okay. I guess I'm stumped."

"Some people come in with laptops and use our Wi-Fi to log onto our network. If whoever you're looking for didn't sign in, I bet they were on Wi-Fi."

"How do we get to who those users were?"

"You can't. I don't have any records, other than a monthly report of use."

"I have days and times. Can I see your video surveillance?"

251

Shelby laughed. "We don't have video surveillance. My budget is barely enough to buy books and pay my salary."

"Thanks for filling me in on the reality of a librarian's life."

"It's not very glamorous, but I knew that when I went to school. Just think, a bachelor's degree and a master's degree in library science, and I'm qualified to do email, schedule volunteers, manage a budget, and answer the phone. My life is not exciting."

I was walking to the SUV when my phone rang. "Fletcher."

"Are you still at the library?" Jess Pond asked. "Your user just logged on to the Somerset library Wi-Fi."

"I just walked out. Thanks."

I jogged back to the library and saw the same three people at the computer desks. I walked through the library and found no one on a laptop, but I did scare a pair of young teens necking in a hidden corner. I powerwalked back to Shelby's office.

"Our suspect is on your Wi-Fi right now, but there's no one in the library on a laptop."

"Our Wi-Fi signal is probably strong enough to be used from the parking lot or street. It might go as far as the building next door."

I nearly ran out of the library. There were only four empty cars in the parking lot, so I walked down the street, looking for someone inside a car staring at their laptop. I checked the bar at the end of the block, then walked back to the pizza café on the opposite corner.

Sitting at a table in the rear was a dark-haired woman engrossed in her laptop computer with a can of Diet Coke in her hand. Her back was to the wall, so no one could see what was on her screen. I pulled out my stack of pictures and found Katie McIvy smiling into the camera. Her hair was a little shorter, but it was her.

I put away my pictures and walked into the café, staying out of her sightline. She jumped when I sat down across from her. I spun the computer and realized I was staring at an email screen.

She jerked the computer away and slammed the lid. "Hey, you can't do that."

I pulled the computer plug and pulled the laptop away from her, setting it on my legs under the table. "Hi, Katie. You've been elusive."

She frowned, staring at my uniform. "This isn't the park. What are you doing here?"

"I'm trying to solve a mystery. Someone's been posting compromising videos of your co-workers on the internet. They've been logging in from the library Wi-Fi."

"I don't know what you're talking about. Give my computer back to me."

"I'm afraid it's evidence, in a case." I pulled out my phone and dialed 911. I identified myself, gave my location, and asked that an officer be dispatched.

"Katie's face blushed, then turned red with anger. "You have no right…"

"You're using your computer in a public establishment. You gave up your right to privacy when you walked in and logged onto a public Wi-Fi. You might've been able to argue that it was private if you'd used the café's network, but you gave it all up when you logged onto the library's Wi-Fi."

My phone buzzed, and I answered.

"Your computer user just shut down the connection."

"I know. I'm the one who shut down the computer."

Jess chuckled. "It's a woman?"

"Yep. Jill warned me it might be."

"Good luck. I'll email the records to you."

Katie glared at me through the conversation. "Who was that?"

"That was the FBI. They've been tracking your computer use and tied the compromising video to your Gmail account. You're busted. Would you care to tell me what's going on?"

"You have to read my rights and offer me an attorney."

"Only if I'm arresting you. Do you want to be arrested, or are you willing to resign from the National Park Service and have this noted on your record if you ever apply for a federal job in the future?"

She slid over to get up. "I'm out of here. Give me my computer."

I grabbed her hand. "Sit there, or I'm going to handcuff you and march you out to the street while we wait for the police."

Katie saw something outside the café that made her blanch. Rather than turning away from her and risking an unpleasant wrestling match while she tried to escape, I sat. The door opened, and Katie's eyes were glued on what I assumed was a cop. I waved my hand without taking my eyes off Katie, and a blue uniform showed up at our table.

A young female officer asked, "Are you Fletcher?"

"Yes, and this is Katie McIvy, who's been posting private videos of her National Park Service co-workers on the internet without permission. She's been using the library Wi-Fi to access the internet."

The Somerset officer, whose nametag said Westin, had Katie scoot over, effectively blocking her into the corner. "So, what are we going to do about this?"

"I'm sure there are federal laws about the transmission of obscene material. What are the Wisconsin laws?"

"Statute 942.09 prohibits the publication or posting of nude material without the prior consent of the subjects. If the co-workers didn't consent to the release of the images, it's illegal."

"What's the penalty for a class I felony, officer Westin?"

"Up to three and a half years in prison and up to a ten-thousand-dollar penalty."

I looked at Katie. "I suppose they'd be lenient in sentencing if you have no prior convictions. But even a year in state prison is a long time for someone your age, and a felony conviction on your criminal record is tough to explain to potential employers."

"Am I under arrest?"

I leaned on the table. "Are we having a discussion here, or are you asking to be handcuffed and read your Miranda rights?"

"What are we discussing?"

"How did you get the video?"

Katie stared at me for a second, then stared into a corner above my head. "My ex-boyfriend had it on his phone."

I glanced at the Somerset officer, and she rolled her eyes.

"Who took the video?"

"My ex-boyfriend before he became my ex."

"Is that why he's your ex-boyfriend?"

Katie nodded.

"Tell me how it got on the internet."

Katie smoldered. "I found it on his phone and emailed it to myself. Then I found the website for cheating ex-whatevers and uploaded it."

"To punish him?"

"No, to fix those two bitches who were prancing around pretending to be…"

"Take it down."

"I don't know how to…"

"You could figure out how to post it, but not how to take it down?"

"You have my computer."

I handed the computer to Katie, and officer Westin watched as Katie punched keys and moved her finger on the computer touchpad. Westin's eyes went wide at one point, and she closely looked at what was on the screen. She glanced at me, giving a look that conveyed whatever she was seeing made her sick.

Katie hit a key and closed the laptop. "It's gone."

I looked at Westin, who nodded.

"Now pull up your email and send your resignation to Cheryl Britten."

Katie glanced at officer Westin, who nodded. She opened the laptop, moved between screens, and started typing. She apparently hit send and closed the laptop again.

"Thank you, Officer Westin," I said, offering my hand as I stood.

"We're good here?"

I nodded and walked her to the door. "How bad was the video?"

Westin waited until a couple walked past. "It was pretty disgusting. If someone had posted something like that featuring one of my friends, I'd probably arrest them and see if the county would press charges. Not many of these cases are making it into the courts, so it's kind of untested water."

I thanked Westin again and walked back into the café. Katie still sat in the back corner with her arms crossed over her chest.

"What happens now?" she asked.

"You'd better start looking for a new job or move home."

"I'm not going to jail?"

I shook my head. "The problem is resolved, and you've been punished. Sadly, there are a bunch of people out there who've seen the video and can't 'unsee' it. There's a chance the performers might want to press civil charges, but that would involve the video being played in court, and I don't think they want that."

Katie picked up her laptop and jammed it into a backpack, then slid out of the corner. She glared at me.

"By the way. The FBI has seen the video, and they know you're the person who posted it. Even though no one is pressing charges, if your name comes up in a federal investigation, this will pop up."

"But I was never arrested or anything."

"Welcome to the internet age, where nothing ever goes away."

I called Jill from the sidewalk and told her to meet me at the park headquarters building. I explained what had happened as I walked to the National Park Service SUV.

"Is that enough punishment, Doug?"

"Sometimes, more punishment is quietly doled out than ever gets to the courtroom."

"But those poor women in the video… If that had been me, I'd want more punishment than having the perpetrator being forced to resign."

"You wouldn't be caught naked in front of a camera."

"No, but still."

"It's over. Pick me up. Where are we going for supper?"

Jill paused. "This is way out of character, but I'd like a burger and fries."

"I saw an old-fashioned malt shop near the Inn."

"That sounds about perfect. I might even split a chocolate malt with you."

"I really like strawberry malts."

Jill laughed. "This is the crunchy versus creamy peanut butter issue all over again. I see a compromise that involves separate malts."

"You won't drink a whole malt. I'll suck it up and we can split a chocolate one."

* * *

We parked around the corner from the malt shop and waited in line for a table. After supper, Jill pushed the last of her fries aside. "The burgers and fries were almost as good as the hand-made malt."

I dipped a pair of her fries in a puddle of ketchup. "Do you want to talk shop?"

She shook her head. "Not tonight."

"Are you excited about being an armed babysitter tomorrow?"

"I'm looking forward to a leisurely canoe trip without searching all of the mosquito-infected backwaters. I hope they put us together in a canoe."

"I doubt that. Cheryl will probably put us in canoes with her experienced rangers. I can't imagine anyone considering either of us competent to sit in the back seat of a canoe on an operation like this."

Jill smirked and wiped her face. "But you're an Eagle Scout with a canoeing merit badge."

"That was a long time ago."

* * *

Jill took a shower, and I turned on the television. A couple of hokey cop shows made me cringe and a situation comedy was dumber than funny, so I turned on CNN and watched a reporter somewhere in the Mideast talk about recent rocket attacks.

Jill was drying her hair and had a towel wrapped around her torso. "Anything about the President's kid on the TV?"

"I'm sure that's a State secret. They wouldn't televise that anymore than they would the route for the Presidential motorcade." I looked up as Jill did the final fluff of her hair. "You look tired."

"Considering we did very little but sit in the car most of the day, it was tiring."

"You probably crashed after your statement to the press."

Jill threw the wet towel at me. "You smartass. If you hadn't pushed me to the microphone, I would've been perfectly happy to stand in the back row, looking professional."

I balled up the towel and tossed it through the open bathroom door. "You did great." I looked at the clock. "Hey, we can probably catch it on the nine o'clock early news."

I turned on the television as Jill picked up her cellphone. The news started as she put a finger in her ear. "Hi, Mom. I thought I'd warn you that I might be on the news tonight..." She walked into the bathroom for the rest of the conversation.

I fell asleep without turning off the television, and I never heard Jill turn it off or get into bed.

Chapter Seventeen

Saturday

Cheryl, the park superintendent, asked us to join the Secret Service briefing. Jill and I slipped into the back of a too-small room jammed with too many people from the Secret Service to the Coast Guard, sheriff's departments, and Natural Resources people from Minnesota and Wisconsin. The Secret Service SAC pushed past Cheryl to the podium.

As you know, the President's son and his class are taking a canoe trip today." He pointed to a map on an easel. "They're going to put their canoes in at the Taylors Falls landing at ten this morning. They're going to paddle to the Osceola Landing, where they're going to stop for lunch. After lunch, they're going to paddle to William O'Brian State Park, where they'll be picked up by the outfitter and bused back to their campground. Our goal is to provide as normal a canoeing experience as possible for the group."

That comment brought a round of chuckles. The SAC put up his hands. "I know that's not possible but work with me to help these kids feel like they're in the wild. I want to blanket this area with protection, but I want it to be invisible to the kids. To that end, the sheriff's boat patrols are on the river, checking the islands and walking the shorelines and bluffs. The Minnesota and Wisconsin Natural Resource Department people will be at every campsite, monitoring the campers. The Coast Guard Reserve will have a boat ahead of the flotilla, clearing the boat traffic. The National Park Service will have a canoe following the flotilla to deal with stragglers and provide first aid. They're also putting a ranger in every other canoe to keep the kids paddling at a sustainable pace, as well as having armed law enforcement rangers in two canoes."

"What's the Secret Service going to do?" an anonymous voice asked from the back of the room.

"We've got the son's personal agent in a canoe alongside him. There's also a helicopter following the flotilla, and we've got sharpshooters at strategic locations along the river." The agent paused. "Any other questions?"

I raised my hand. "Have you received any credible threats?"

"We have no specific threats, but we always act out of an abundance of caution. If there's nothing else, my agents will work with your people to implement the plan."

The local law enforcement people melted away, except for the SAC, Cheryl, Jill, and me. "Where do you want us, Cheryl?"

"My rangers are spread paper-thin. I split you two between the lead and trailing canoes."

The Secret Service agent looked at Jill's badge and firearm. "Have you ever qualified with that firearm, Ranger Fletcher?"

Jill was surprised by the question. "As a matter of fact, I'm a National Park Service investigator, and I've not only qualified with my weapon, I've fired it in the line of duty. Have you?"

The SAC smiled. "Did you put down a rabid gopher?"

Jill was about to tee off on him when I stepped forward. "She's been involved in two undercover operations that ended in gunfire. In one, Jill fired at a suspect while other law enforcement people sought cover."

"Ah, you provided covering fire."

Jill got into the guy's personal space. "I fired at a running suspect and hit him with thirteen shots while FBI agents were running for cover."

Cheryl pushed forward to de-escalate the confrontation. "Doug and Jill are two of our most seasoned law enforcement people. Each of them has been in several gunfights and won commendations. If you're ever in a shooting situation, you'd do well to have one of them backing you up."

The Secret Service SAC looked skeptical but didn't pursue the confrontation. "We've got canoes from the National Park Service and an outfitter. On Cheryl's suggestion, I've put a ranger in the rear of each canoe and an armed agent in the front. Check the postings to see who you're with."

Jill and I walked to a whiteboard. The canoes were numbered, and the pairings named with their agencies listed. The most experienced canoeists were National Park Service rangers and the outfitter's guides.

"You've got to be kidding," I said when I saw my name listed as the experienced person in the back of a canoe with a female Secret Service agent. "This week is the first time I've been in a canoe in thirty years. I'm experienced?"

Cheryl stood next to me and looked through the list. "Doug, experience is relative. Compared to the Secret Service agents, you're a pro."

"You're scraping the bottom of the barrel if I'm one of your 'experienced canoeists.'"

Jill found her name as the front passenger, teamed with one of the outfitter's guides. She smiled. "I'm okay with my partner."

Cheryl herded us aside. "You guys are from the Midwest, so you'll get this. The Secret Service guy is from the East Coast, and he's clueless. The weather report is for thunderstorms boiling up this afternoon. We should be off the water before they hit, but if this flotilla doesn't get going on time, or if people dawdle, we're going to have problems. Doug, I want you at the back of the pack to make sure the stragglers keep moving along. Jill, I've got you in the canoe next to the head

Secret Service guy. If this storm comes in early, you'll need to prod him and make sure his people aren't slowing things down for security reasons to the point where the whole bunch of you get caught on the water when the storms hit."

"Why me?" Jill asked.

"Because you're the senior National Park Service person on the water. He's already expressed derision at the youth and inexperience of my rangers. You've got experience and credentials that may influence him to listen to your input."

We walked outside, and I handed Jill a bottle of insect repellent. I slathered 70 SPF sunscreen on my arms and face. "Are you okay with this arrangement?"

We swapped bottles, and Jill covered her legs with sunscreen. "Not really. We're taking a five-plus hour canoe trip. If the weather forecast is wrong, or if we get slowed down..."

"Yeah. It's not our show, and all we can do is play our parts."

Jill considered that. "I'm not risking my life in a lightning storm because some bureaucrat doesn't understand the danger of a thunderstorm."

"Once we get past the halfway point, there is a scout camp or a Catholic retreat where we can take shelter, plus a lot of little backwater islands to hide on."

Jill handed the sunscreen back to me and pulled me close. "I'll be in the front and will hit those shelters a lot sooner than you. Promise me you'll take care of yourself."

"I'm not going to worry about it. Thunderstorms are a late afternoon and evening event in this region. We've got plenty of time to get off the river."

Jill looked into my eyes. "That's not what I asked of you."

"Okay, I'll take care of myself. I promise."

Jill turned and took a step when a bird's shadow crossed between us. A fraction of a second later a white blob struck her shoulder. She spun around, thinking I'd tapped her. "What?"

"Um, a bird got you?"

"What do you mean?"

"Look at your shoulder."

Jill turned her head and pulled her shirt. "Great. Just the icing on the cake." She pulled a tissue from her pocket and wiped her shirt, removing most of the solids but leaving a white stain.

I suppressed a smile. "It's better but not gone. The rain should wash it clean."

Her withering glare told me that might not have been the perfect response. After a moment's hesitation Jill walked up to me and stuck her finger in my face as her other hand delivered the dirty tissue to my pants pocket. "You can deal with that...dear."

* * *

The launch was a zoo. There were more armed people than the group of Washington D.C. teens who were being protected. That didn't include the people along the river as snipers, and the Coast Guard and local water patrol people deployed closer to Stillwater. The St. Croix narrowed and ran between steep rock walls through the dells area. The river was swollen by melted snow in the spring, and the dells area was a challenging canoe course. In July, the river was down to "normal," but the current between the steep escarpments was still stronger than the lower part of the river, where it became gentler. The strong current made the canoe loading a challenge for the inexperienced teens and many of the Secret Service agents. The outfitters held the canoes and assisted with the loading, but a couple of canoes nearly tipped over during the process. Others pushed off and got broadside in the current, creating a few tense moments rocking before getting oriented downstream.

I waved to Jill as she stepped spritely into a green canoe with a male outfitter, who looked like he was eighteen. Her deeply tanned guide was well muscled. They paddled away, her "expert" taking deep, powerful strokes. Between him and the orange life vest, I felt good about Jill's situation and safety.

My partner hung back with several other Secret Service agents. "Hi, I'm Doug Fletcher."

Secret Service Agent Augusta Smith was thirtyish, looked like a no-nonsense cop with short brown hair under her floppy wide-brimmed hat. She was in better shape than me but was what the locals call "fish-belly white" from hours in a uniform, shielded from the sun. She put out her hand and introduced herself by her first name, which put me somewhat at ease.

I handed her the sunscreen. "Doug Fletcher."

She glanced at the pistol on my hip but didn't comment. "I was looking forward to getting a little tan."

"We're going to be on the water for over five hours. If you don't use sunscreen, you'll be blistered by the time we're through."

She skeptically looked at me.

"Believe me. I've been there. I came home from a camping trip and had to soak in a bathtub to take off my t-shirt because the blisters broke and glued it to my skin."

"Thanks," she said, taking the bottle. "We're all in civvies, so can't tell what agency you're with?"

"National Park Service."

She visibly relaxed. "So, you know how to paddle a canoe."

"I'm a little rusty, but I'm experienced. I take it you haven't spent much time in a canoe."

"I'm not a water person." She nodded at the holster on my hip. "You're not one of the local rangers."

"I'm a National Park Service investigator." I handed her the bottle of insect repellent.

"What's this for?"

"If we get out of the main channel, we'll get eaten alive by the mosquitoes. If we beach the canoe in a secluded grassy area, there'll be deer ticks."

Augusta sniffed the insect repellent and tried to hand it back. "I'll take my chances with an itchy mosquito bite."

"First of all, the mosquitoes here are the size of Piper Cubs, and they'll suck you dry like a vampire in about an hour. Secondly, the mosquitoes sometimes carry equine encephalitis, and the deer ticks carry Lyme disease."

Augusta took the insect repellent and sprayed herself. "Are you based here?"

"Two of us were brought in from North Padre Island National Seashore."

"I don't detect a Texas accent."

"I grew up in Minnesota. I was a St. Paul cop before the National Park Service hired me."

Augusta smiled. "You're a 'real' cop, so I don't have to worry about you shooting me in the back of the head."

I laughed. "I promise to not shoot you anywhere."

The outfitter who was coordinating the canoe loading called out our names. We were in one of the two last canoes. Jill and her partner had disappeared around a river bend, and the group of teens was nearly out of sight. We strapped on orange life vests, and Augusta stepped into the canoe, making it rock and nearly dumping her into the river. I carefully put my foot into the middle of the canoe, keeping my center of gravity low. I took the paddle from the kid who was helping us, and he pushed us off.

Augusta took dainty dabs with her paddle, leaving me to take deeper strokes to get us moving toward the back of the canoe ahead of us. I used muscles that had been idle for years and struggled to make strokes that kept us going straight. Augusta randomly switched which side she paddled on as she tired, causing me to adjust so the canoe kept going in a straight line.

"Let me know when you're going to switch sides so I can compensate."

Augusta looked over her shoulder. "Sorry, I didn't know I was messing you up. It seems like we're going in a straight line."

I stopped paddling and let her take three strokes on the right side that pushed us sharply left. "Oh," she said over her shoulder.

We quickly caught up to the last canoe, and the pace slowed. The current carried us along almost as fast as the last of the teen group, so I only made easy strokes, mostly to keep us going straight. The last of the teen canoes, had an overweight guy and a spindly girl who were falling behind. I took a couple of deep strokes and pulled alongside them.

"Pick up your pace a little. We need to keep up with the group."

The overweight, sweaty boy was not adept at paddling, having to alternate his strokes between the sides of the canoe to cut a zigzag course down the river.

"Watch me," I said, demonstrating a J-stroke that powered us ahead but ended with a twist of the paddle that corrected for overpowering the paddler in the front. After a couple of attempts, the kid caught on, and they made better headway on a straighter path.

I pushed ahead a little further and encouraged the skinny girl to dig her paddle a little deeper and use her back muscles instead of just her arms to power the paddle. As they picked up speed, I stopped paddling and fell in behind them.

Augusta twisted her head. "That was good. You actually know what you're doing."

"It's like riding a bike. The first block is wobbly, but your muscles remember what to do after a little while."

A canoe with two of the twentyish outfitter's guides pulled alongside us. Their easy strokes made me feel like I was dog paddling alongside an Olympic swimmer.

The paddler in the back, with the bleached blond look of a surfer, eased next to me. "You guys look like you're doing good." I sensed that he wanted to add *for an old guy.*

"We're fine. What's your role in this?"

"In a bike marathon, we'd be called the 'sag wagon.' If anyone gets blisters, loses a paddle, or just can't go on, we're here to help."

I gave them a thumbs up sign, and they eased in behind us.

Our slow pokes caught up to the next to last teen canoe. But the group had strung out so far that the lead canoes were mostly out of sight. I watched the paddlers in the two trailing canoes. They were inexperienced and out of shape. No amount of encouragement or paddling tips were going to catch them up. I resigned myself to the role of keeping them moving along.

Augusta looked over her shoulder. "I'm supposed to be protecting Rabbit, not babysitting his slow buddies."

"Who's Rabbit?"

"All the First Family have nicknames. The son is 'Rabbit.'"

"Dare I ask why?"

"He's on his high school cross-country running team. 'Quick as a bunny.'"

"I was told to stay with the back of the pack so we don't lose anyone."

"I think we should catch up with the Secret Service coverage team. The sag wagon guys can keep an eye on the stragglers."

"Those aren't my orders."

Augusta set her paddle across the gunwales and dug in a waterproof bag. She pulled out a radio and announced our situation, asking for guidance.

A male voice responded. "Leave the stragglers with the outfitter's people. You're supposed to be providing the rear of the personal protection coverage."

Augusta turned. "Did you get that?"

"Loud and clear. You do know it's going to take us half an hour to catch up with that next group. It's not like pressing the accelerator in a drag racer."

"Make it happen."

I waved to the outfitter's canoe, and they shot forward like a greyhound. "We got orders to move ahead to the next group. You guys are covering the stragglers."

"Roger that."

Augusta didn't stow her radio in her waterproof bag, which I thought was a poor choice. She dug in with her paddle, showing more energy than I'd seen before. We pulled ahead of the two canoes of stragglers. We were less than an hour into the trip, and they already looked spent. The sag wagon crew had their work cut out for them.

The group ahead was out of sight, and we were a hundred yards ahead of the stragglers. We got to a straight stretch of river, and I could see the long string of canoes ahead. Although we were paddling hard, we made minimal headway catching up to the back of the pack. My back muscles already burned, and Augusta's surge waned.

"We're not going to catch up for a while. Use your back. Pace yourself."

Augusta's strokes became more even, and they came from her shoulders and back instead of from her arms. I ensured we were in the strongest current to get the most benefit from its power.

Chapter Eighteen

After what seemed like an hour, we were still hundreds of yards behind the main group of canoes. I pulled in my paddle and took a bottle of water from the dry pack the outfitters had given each of us. "Take a break. Open your water and take a drink."

She set her paddle across the gunwales and rolled her shoulders. "This looks so easy, but it's a workout," she said as she opened her water.

I straightened my bad knee and flexed it, then unwrapped a candy bar and took a bite. "You'll know how much of a workout this was tomorrow when your back and arms are screaming at you. Take a bite of the candy bar. You're burning calories like mad."

"Yeah, I won't need to hit the gym in the hotel tonight." She ate her candy bar and stowed the wrapper in the bag. "Is the woman in the front canoe your wife?"

"Yes," I replied, capping my water and putting it away. "We work investigations out of Padre Island National Seashore."

"Texas? Not Washington?"

"If they transferred us to Washington, they'd be hiring two new investigators."

We started paddling again at a sustainable pace. "Washington's not so bad."

"I couldn't afford the rent and don't want to be around that many people. Plus, I don't want to be that close to the bosses. Texas is fine."

We made small talk for another hour as we slowly closed the gap to the group ahead of us. I'd been watching the sky, and the clouds were becoming puffy with tall tops, a harbinger of the upcoming thunderstorm. I checked my watch, and we were still hours away from the park where the outfitter would pick us up.

"I don't like the look of the clouds."

"They're puffy. Is that bad?"

"It takes really tall clouds to make hail, and the ones off to our west are ominous."

Augusta picked up the pace of her paddling. "Should I be worried?"

"Not yet, but if they start turning dark or if we hear thunder, you should worry."

We neared the back of the pack when we passed under the Osceola bridge, which was about the halfway point of the trip. The sides of the river had dropped down after exiting the dells area, so the current slowed. We encountered islands and the side channels we'd explored during the investigation. A Coast Guard boat was visible far ahead of us, near Jill's canoe.

Augusta saw the boat about the same time. "We're past the really dangerous part of the trip."

"How do you figure?"

"The Secret Service was anxious about the difficulty in providing protection in the river with the steep rock sides. We couldn't check all the nooks and crannies where a sniper could hide. It's easier to sweep the shoreline here, and we've got boats that can respond to a threat much faster than the canoes."

The words were hardly out of her mouth when I felt as much as heard the first rumble of thunder. "Uh, oh."

She looked over her shoulder. "Was that a truck?"

"That was thunder. Get on your radio and find out what's going on."

Augusta reached for the radio when the Coast Guard boat spun around and eased into the middle of the canoe pack.

"Rabbit is secure. We're taking him to the alternate exit location."

The extraction took place a couple of hundred meters ahead of us, and then the boat eased away without causing a wake. It motored a distance in front of the canoes, then the operator opened the throttle, and the boat rose in the water and sped away.

"So, that's it?" I asked. "The President's kid gets whisked away at the first sound of thunder, and the rest of us are left to fend for ourselves?"

Augusta looked over her shoulder and smiled. "Welcome to the Secret Service. We are mission-driven, and our mission is to protect Rabbit."

"What about the other seventeen kids and the thirty of us milling around them?"

"They are now in the hands of the National Park Service and other agencies."

"Where is 'the alternate extraction point?'"

"The scout camp across the river from Stillwater only has one entrance road. We secured it this morning and locked it down in case there was an emergency like this."

The thunder rumbled again, this time more sustained and much louder. More boats appeared. I assumed they were from the local counties and the Minnesota and Wisconsin Departments of Natural Resources. They started loading teens out of the canoes and into the boats, tying the canoes on behind. There weren't enough boats to evacuate all the people in the canoes ahead of us, and they seemed to be prioritizing the extraction of the remaining teens.

"At least they'll get the kids out of here," I said and looked back. The two canoes of teens with the outfitters weren't visible. "Shit, the stragglers aren't even in sight."

The radio came to life. "The storm is about a half-hour away. There are campgrounds and landings ahead. Everyone, get off the river at your first opportunity and radio in your location for land pickup."

Augusta looked over her shoulder. "If you can pinpoint where we are, I'll look at the National Park Service map and see where we can get out."

I dug my paddle in the water and back paddled, turning the bow upstream. "We're going back to help the stragglers. Paddle!"

Augusta didn't pick up her paddle. "We were just told to take shelter."

"Augusta, the canoes behind us don't have a radio, and they have no idea how close the storm is."

Augusta picked up the radio and announced our intention to circle back for the last of the group. Then she turned off the radio and put it in the waterproof bag.

"You shut off the radio?" I asked as she dug her paddle deep into the water.

"Hell, yes! They're going to repeat the order to take shelter, and now I can say I didn't hear it rather than having to admit I was insubordinate."

"Hey, you're okay, for a fed."

"Fletcher, you're a fed, too."

"By the way, my name is Doug. It's reassuring to hear someone admit that the National Park Service is part of the federal government. I thought the only time anyone admitted that was when it came time for budget cuts and furloughs."

"Shut up and paddle, Doug."

The thunder was nearly a continuous bass rumble, punctuated by the sharper crack of lightning. We came around the tip of an island and saw the three canoes in the rear a few hundred meters behind us. They were paddling hard with the aid of the current, and the distance between us was closing rapidly.

The wind picked up ahead of the rain, and the placid water turned into waves, lapping at the stern of the canoe and spraying my back. A gust caught Augusta's floppy hat and blew it into the water ahead of us, where it sank under a wave. A flash of lightning hit somewhere ashore, and I counted off the seconds between the flash and the thunder.

Augusta flinched. "That was too close."

"I counted about ten seconds between the flash and the thunder, so still two miles away."

She furiously paddled. "Are you blowing smoke up my butt?"

"No. There's a five-second delay between the lightning and thunder for every mile you're away from the strike."

We were within thirty meters of the stragglers when the front outfitter waved toward the east. The two canoes of teens turned toward a narrow channel between two islands.

I gently eased the canoe to the right, so the waves were quartering into the back of the bow, pushing us ahead but rolling us slightly with each wave. One of the canoes turned too quickly, and waves hit it directly on the side. It rocked with each wave. I recognized the fat kid and skinny girl and saw the terror on the girl's face as the canoe rolled. We were near the channel when their canoe capsized, throwing them into the churning water.

Lightning flashed, followed two seconds later by the boom. Augusta dug her paddle deep into the water and recited Hail Mary's. The outfitters reached the capsized canoe before we did. They gestured for us to follow the other two stragglers into the narrow channel while they struggled with the two teens in the water. The small island blocked the waves. I took a deep breath, reassured we wouldn't have to swim to shore.

I heard the rain coming and eased the bow of the canoe onto the sandy shore. When I glanced back to check on the outfitters, I saw the sheet of rain progressing across the river. Within seconds, the other shore disappeared, and pouring rain drenched us.

I jumped out of the canoe and pushed it ashore as the two teens jumped out. They took a few running steps toward the two large trees on the little spit of sand.

"No! Don't stand under the trees during the lightning!"

My words were lost in the wind and pounding rain. Augusta was ready to follow them but heard me and stopped. "So, what do we do?"

"Lie down away from the canoe."

I looked back toward the river and saw the orange of life jackets coming toward us. The two outfitters were swimming the two teens from the capsized canoe toward shore. I waded out until chest-deep then reached out and grabbed the skinny girl's arm. I pulled her close, and we struggled to shore together with her coughing up the river water swallowed while the waves smashed her and her partner. I pushed her to Augusta, who'd followed me into the water, then I grabbed the other teen as the outfitters jumped out of their canoe into the waist deep water.

We scrambled ashore and got everyone on the ground as a blinding flash of lightning hit so close that the sound nearly deafened me, and a shockwave knocked me to the ground. A shower of splinters followed. Bending low, I trotted toward the trees where the first teens had taken shelter. They were both lying on the ground in crumpled heaps. I threw myself down next to a girl with brown hair matted to her face. When I put my fingers on her neck to check for a pulse, her eyes fluttered open.

"Who are you?" she croaked.

"I'm Doug. Can you feel your hands and feet?"

She stared at me for a second, then squeezed her hands into fists and wiggled her toes. "Yeah."

I crawled on hands and knees to the other teen, a boy with deep acne and his hair in cornrows. I touched his neck and couldn't feel a pulse. I rolled him onto his back and started chest compressions.

I felt a presence at my elbow, and one of the outfitters pushed me aside. "I'm an EMT. I've got this. You might be able to get cell service here. Call 911."

I scrambled back to the canoes where the two girls were now huddled with Augusta. The other outfitter and the chubby kid sat next to them.

"Augusta, see if you can raise someone on your radio. The kid under the tree needs medical assistance. I'll try my cellphone."

Out of reflex, I reached in my pants pocket for my cell, then realized I'd stowed it in the waterproof bag.

I tried to shake the water off my hands before opening the bag. The other outfitter grabbed my arm. "My phone's waterproof. I'll call."

Augusta was on her radio but not getting a response through the crackling interference caused by the lightning. Another bolt of lightning hit nearby, causing us all to fall to the ground. It hit so close I felt tingling in my feet.

The waterproof phone worked because there was an animated discussion from both sides yelling to be heard over the pounding rain. I sat down next to Augusta, who'd given up on her radio when the phone call connected. She looked blurred through the water running over my eyes.

"Are you okay?" I asked.

She nodded, then looked toward the EMT, who continued chest compressions.

"You might want to continue your Hail Mary's for a while."

Augusta shook her head. "I've never seen anyone survive if they didn't get cardioversion within a couple minutes from the start of CPR. Nobody's going to be here quickly enough to save that kid."

I stood up. The lightning had passed us. "Doesn't mean you shouldn't say Hail Mary's." I walked back to the EMT. "Take a break. I'll take a shift."

He leaned away, letting me take over. "Did you get through on your phone?"

"Your partner was talking to dispatch. I don't know what they told him."

"Are you okay continuing CPR while I ask him what's happening?"

I nodded.

He came back and knelt beside me, putting his fingers on the teen's neck. After a few seconds, he put his hand on my arm and shook his head. He had tears in his eyes. "They won't put anyone on the water if there's lightning within two miles. No one's going to be here in the next half-hour."

I leaned back and drew in a deep breath. The rain eased from the deluge to a pleasant shower. Augusta walked to us and knelt next to the dead teen. She put her hand over the kid's eyes and bowed her head, apparently saying a silent prayer. She seemed surprised that we were all staring at her.

"What?"

"We're all praying with you," I said.

The other three teens walked toward us. Augusta got up and herded them back toward the canoes. I looked at the outfitter, who'd done the CPR and was now spent. "You tried, but I don't think he ever had a chance." I pointed to the teen's shoes. "The lightning blew the soles off his sneakers."

* * *

The Coast Guard found us about two hours later. They brought a blue tarp, and we wrapped the body and loaded him onto the boat. We got onto their boat and tied the canoes behind. They took us to a marina north of Stillwater, where we were met by an ambulance, several police cars, and a National Park Service pickup. I could see Jill standing back from the crowd, looking apprehensive. She was searching the faces on the boat, apparently getting the news that one of the canoeists had died, but no one had given a name.

When her eyes met mine, she wrapped her arms around herself and broke into tears. She sobbed for a few seconds, then walked onto the dock with the rest of the people welcoming us. I helped the teens off the boat, then Augusta and I helped lift the body onto the dock.

When I stepped on the dock, Jill timidly walked over, almost like she was afraid to see if I'd been injured. I pulled her into my arms. "I promised I'd take care of myself."

She nodded, burying her head in my shoulder. Then she stepped back and buried a knuckle into my ribs.

"Ouch! Why did you do that?"

285

"So help me, if you ever scare me like this again, I'll break one of your ribs." She grabbed my hand and pulled me down the dock. "You smell like dead fish and slime. The Inn will probably want to hose you down outside the kitchen before they let you up to our room."

"Yeah, I could probably use a shower and some fresh clothes."

"I'm not sure just a shower will do it. I may have to buy a gallon of bleach and a scrub brush at the hardware store." She held the passenger door of the National Park Service pickup for me.

"Where's the rental car?"

"It's still at the park headquarters. Besides, the rental agency probably has a cleaning upcharge for situations like this."

We drove in silence to the Inn. Jill followed me through the lobby where we got curious looks from the man at the desk and the two guests waiting to be seated in the dining room. Once in our room, I stripped off my sodden clothes in the bathroom and pushed them into a corner.

Jill, still very shy, watched. "I'm surprised a fish didn't fall out of your pants when you pulled them down."

I stepped into the shower. "No fish. Just algae slime."

"What happened out there?" She asked, raising her voice to be heard over the shower.

"It's kind of a long story. Let's talk over supper."

I nearly fell when the shower curtain opened unexpectedly. To my utter surprise, Jill stepped in with a washcloth.

She spun me around so I was facing away and took the soap out of my hand. "I'll scrub your back. There's no way the dining room will let you in until every square inch of your skin has been scrubbed until it's pink."

I turned around and pulled her close. "Work on this side now."

She put her head against my shoulder, and I could feel her sob as the water poured over us. "I thought you were dead."

I patted her back and held her close. When she was breathing normally, I turned off the water and stepped onto the bathmat. I handed her a towel and then dried myself off.

She wrapped the towel around herself and walked into the bedroom. When I walked out of the bathroom, she was dressed in a blouse and shorts. She ran her fingers through her hair and sat on the bed.

"Cheryl's meeting us in the dining room."

"When?"

"She's probably waiting for us now."

* * *

Cheryl sat at a table with a glass of red wine and three menus. She got up and hugged Jill, then me. She appeared shellshocked.

"Well, it was quite a day. The Secret Service is gone. My boss called to ream me for losing a guest." She looked at me. "I'd

287

appreciate it if you'd write up a report about what happened."

"No problem."

She signaled for the waitress, who nearly trotted over. "Are your guests ready for a beverage?"

Jill ordered wine. I was too wound up to drink, so I ordered a tonic and lime.

"That's it, Doug? I thought you'd have a double Johnny Walker or something after today."

"It's days like today that made me give up Johnny Walker." I replayed the afternoon for Jill and Cheryl, had a nice rib-eye steak, and sipped on my tonic while Cheryl and Jill drank a second glass of wine.

Cheryl, a little tipsy, reached out and took both our hands. "Thank you." She teared up, wiped her mouth with her napkin, and got up. "The bill for dinner and your room is paid."

Jill and I walked upstairs to our room, and Jill hung the do not disturb sign outside the door.

"Do you think that's necessary?" I asked.

She pressed her back against the door and took a deep breath. "You keep saying we should treat every day like there might not be a tomorrow."

"So?"

"I'm emotionally at the brink, and I need to be with the one I love. Do you think you can handle that duty?"

288

"I can talk, snuggle, cuddle, whatever you need."

Jill put her hand on my chest. "I just want to lie next to you and listen to your heartbeat for a while."

She crawled into bed and rested her ear against my chest. I thought she'd fallen asleep, and then her hand slipped down my abdomen.

"Were you injured by the lightning strike?"

"My feet tingled for a bit, but I don't have any permanent injuries."

She slid her hand inside the elastic of my boxers. "So, all the parts down here are functional?"

"I'm pretty sure they're uninjured, but we can check them out."

Jill squirmed around, gliding her naked body against me. "One part seems to be working, or else there's a banana in your boxers."

Chapter Nineteen

Sunday

With the investigation complete, our airline tickets non-refundable, and a day to kill in the Twin Cities, I reluctantly called my mother for the details of the family reunion. As soon as the stores opened, Jill went shopping in Stillwater and found a cute summer dress and sandals. Taking a hint from her Texas friend, Mandy, she bought some tasteful makeup (something she didn't need, and was loathe to wear) and underwear to make her more curvaceous.

While Jill shopped, I killed the morning by updating Mark Guertin, the Stillwater Police Chief, on the previous day and talking Cheryl Britton through the incident report required when a National Park Service guest was severely injured or died. Those duties complete, I went to the lobby, got a cup of coffee, and bought a newspaper. The events on the river received front page coverage on a corner below the fold. My name didn't show up, which was perfect. The outfitters were given credit for the rescue during the storm, and the attempt to save the boy struck by lightning, which was where the credit belonged.

Jill came into the room carrying a handful of shopping bags and disappeared into the bathroom. A little while later, she walked out and twirled around. "What do you think?"

I set aside the newspaper and was at a loss for words.

"I take it that means you approve?"

Her tomboy 'I'm going to outcompete every man I meet' look was gone. I knew better than to bring up those observations. "You're going to turn heads."

She smiled, and her dimples told me how pleased she was with the compliment. "Your turn for the bathroom."

I pulled her into my arms. "Let's skip the family reunion. This is our honeymoon."

She pushed me hard enough to create a buffer. "I'm happy that you approve of my outfit, but I'm looking forward to actually meeting some of your family."

I picked up the fresh clothes I'd set on the bed and walked to the bathroom. "You may regret that choice."

* * *

We drove across Highway 36 toward the Como Park Zoo complex, the venue an uncle had reserved for the two hundred or so cousins, children, and significant others expected to attend the reunion. I turned south on Lexington and slowed as we drove past a strip mall with a Dairy Queen that had been there as long as I could remember.

"Last chance to back out. I can circle through the parking lot, get onto the highway, and drive back to Stillwater."

"Are you embarrassed about me?"

I laughed. "No. I'm more worried that one of my cousins or uncles will hit on you, and it'll cause a scene when I punch them."

"I can defend myself. You don't need to punch anyone."

I thought back to her effective use of knuckles to the solar plexus and elbows to the ribs and agreed that she was fully capable of defending herself.

I parked near the reunion pavilion, and we walked arm in arm down the sidewalk. As expected, hundreds of people were there, most of whom I didn't recognize and apparently, they didn't remember me. The smoky haze of grilling meats hung in the air, and a hundred conversations buzzed in the background.

"Doug! Over here!" I turned toward the shouts and saw my cousin Eleanor waving. Standing next to her was her husband and two other people who looked vaguely familiar.

"Hi, El. Do you remember Jill from your Flagstaff visit?"

I could tell from El's expression that she didn't. In her defense, the last time she'd seen Jill, we'd been at the Flagstaff airport. Jill wore a National Park Service uniform, had long salt and pepper hair in a ponytail, and wasn't wearing makeup.

Jill stepped forward and hugged Eleanor. "It's so nice to see you again."

El lifted Jill's hand and inspected the wedding ring. "That's lovely, Jill." El hugged me. "And, Doug, you look younger and happier."

Jill hugged Todd and was congratulated on our wedding. Todd leaned close and in a stage-whisper, he said, "Look out for Doug's lecherous uncle, Tom. He's sixty and is married to a college coed. He's notorious for ogling and groping pretty women."

Jill smiled. "Bring him on. I took a self-defense course, and I'll give him a bruise that'll last for weeks."

El's eyes sparkled. "I believe you could do that."

"Oh, I can."

"Yoo-hoo. Jill, over here!"

I thought it was funny that my mother would yell out Jill's name rather than mine, but they'd bonded over our previous meetings, and Mom left me with the impression I'd become superfluous to their relationship. I viewed that as a good thing, much better than the animosity

I'd seen other people display toward their in-laws.

Mom hugged Jill, Todd, and then Eleanor. She kissed my cheek, then grabbed Jill's hand, and they disappeared into the crowd.

El looked shocked. "I take it that Jill's won over Aunt Ronnie."

"It seems that way."

Todd grabbed my elbow. "The beer and pop are in coolers over here." When we were away from Eleanor, he stopped and earnestly looked at me. "I hardly recognized Jill. Ronnie told us Jill was a little older than you, not that it matters, but I wouldn't have guessed she was a day over thirty-five."

I smiled. "I appreciate you not telling her that, but she'll be pleased when I tell her someone guessed that she was thirty-five."

"She's also charming and self-confident. I'm..."

"Surprised that she's putting up with cynical old me?"

Todd smiled but didn't answer.

"We've worked to carve out our relationship, but once we'd found common ground...it's been incredible. There have been some bumps, but we're both smart enough to know it's worth investing the time and effort to make our marriage work."

"Tell me about it. I'm married to Ms. Vegan, and I have to sneak in a burger occasionally to exert my independence."

Todd and I found coolers of iced drinks, and I took out a Diet Coke. Todd opened a beer and steered me around the pavilion, reintroducing me to long-lost cousins. Someone announced that lunch was ready.

I looked for Mom and Jill but gave up and got in the food line with Eleanor and Todd. El loaded a plate with raw vegetables, skipping the ranch dip that contained buttermilk. Todd and I piled sauerkraut on grilled bratwurst, garnering a disapproving look from Eleanor.

I was throwing my paper plate and napkin into a trash can when I felt a hand on my elbow.

"Doug, how have you been?" my Aunt Mary asked.

I hugged Mary, my mother's youngest sister, who happened to be about the same age as Jill. "I'm well, thank you."

"Ronnie introduced me to Jill. She seems nice. And you seem happier than I've ever seen you."

"Thanks, I'm happier than I've been in years."

"You deserve a little happiness after ridding yourself of the college professor leech."

I was shocked by Mary's comment. "Was it that obvious?"

Mary nodded. "She sucked everything out of you and left you empty. It appears Jill is helping you heal." She patted my arm and walked away.

Jill slipped her arm around my waist. "I overheard that discussion. You've been much more reserved than your aunt when commenting about your ex-wife."

"There's nothing to gain by throwing dirt on her." I looked around the crowd and didn't see anyone I knew or wanted to talk to. "Are you ready to go?"

"I think so. I've met a cross-section of your family. Most of them are nice and polite."

I raised my eyebrows. "Some weren't?"

Jill smiled. "Your Uncle Tom has a bruised rib."

I hooked Jill's arm and walked back to the car without saying goodbye to anyone. I drove around Como Lake and through the local neighborhoods I'd known since childhood. People were having picnics on blankets spread near the lake, and we passed groups of joggers and bicyclists.

Jill watched out the side window. "St. Paul is nice. I could live here."

"Maybe in the summer. It's a frozen wasteland in the winter."

"Really? People bragged about the Winter Carnival and suggested we come back in January."

"Think of the coldest South Dakota days, only without the wind, then envision thousands of people standing on the sidewalk watching a parade. That's one day out of a long winter. There's no way I'm coming back here in January unless someone's holding a gun on me."

"But there is hockey, basketball, museums, concerts in both St. Paul and Minneapolis, plays, restaurants, and more."

"I'm at a point in my life where I'd rather stay at home with you and ride my bike on the beach. I don't need to be around a crowd any larger than Matt, Mandy, and you."

I parked in the ramp next to the Inn, and we walked through the lobby. An older gentleman was checking in. He turned to watch Jill walk by, then looked at me and gave me a smile that said he was sure I was having a fling or a tryst with a younger woman.

I closed the door to our room, and Jill hugged me and buried her head in my shoulder. "Thanks for indulging me and taking me to the reunion. It was nice to see Ronnie, and she was pleased to introduce me to your family."

"She wasn't 'introducing you to my family,' she was showing you off."

Jill smiled. "I know. It was flattering. No one's ever shown me off before."

"A cousin told me I was a cradle robber. He was sure you weren't a day over thirty-five."

"Bull."

"Really. You look stupendous."

Jill's eyes moistened, and she pulled me close. "No one ever says…"

I held her and stroked her hair. "Shh. Your tomboy days are long gone. You're the swan now."

"No one said things like that unless they were trying to get me into their bed." She paused, then stepped back a bit and started unbuttoning my shirt. "I never fell for those lines until you came along. I've got years of celibacy to make up for. Are you prepared to help?"

"I might be up to the task."

The End

2019 Bestselling Author
Dean L. Hovey

Dean Hovey is the bestselling and award-winning author of the Doug Fletcher mysteries, the Whistling Pines cozies, and the Pine County mysteries. His research, travel, and scientific background bring richness to his stories. One reviewer said, "His characters are people I'd like to meet over a couple of beers."

Dean and his wife split their year between northern Minnesota and Arizona.

BWL Publishing

bwlpublishing.ca